THE GUNSMITH

445

The Curse of the Gold City

Books by J.R. Roberts
(Robert J. Randisi)

The Gunsmith series

Lady Gunsmith series

Angel Eyes series

Tracker series

Mountain Jack Pike series

COMING SOON!

The Gunsmith
446 – Deadville City

For more information visit:
www.SpeakingVolumes.us

THE GUNSMITH

445

The Curse of the Gold City

J.R. Roberts

SPEAKING VOLUMES, LLC
NAPLES, FLORIDA
2019

The Curse of the Gold City

ISBN 978-1-64540-005-9

Chapter One

San Francisco

THE CURSE OF THE GOLD CITY. It was the headline he had read in the *San Francisco Chronicle*.

Denver usually satisfied Clint Adams' urges for time in a big city, but on the occasions that it didn't fit the bill, he would go to either New York, Chicago or San Francisco. This time it was San Francisco.

While in the city, most of his time was usually spent in the Portsmouth Square hotels and gambling casinos. He had been staying at the new Palladium Hotel in the square when, one morning while having breakfast in the dining room, he saw the headline in the Post. It caught his attention.

Usually, he was interested in either gambling, theater, women, or all three. But this intrigued him.

The article said a famous explorer and Professor of Archeology was in town to give a lecture about his latest venture, which was a trip to India to excavate a newly discovered Tomb. Clint had traveled to many places—all parts of the United States, as well as other countries—including South America, England and Australia. However, he had never been to India and, in fact, had never even thought about it.

Normally, Clint wasn't very interested in lectures. They were dry and boring. But this one sounded like it could be interesting. He scanned the article for the location, saw that it was taking place at a museum on Market Street the next day.

The woman in bed next to him stirred. He had managed to get out of bed and collect the newspaper from the hall without waking her. Now, she turned over onto her back and stretched. The sheet covered her full body, so he set the newspaper down on the floor and slid the sheet down so that her breasts were bare. She was a busty woman in her late thirties who he had met in the Rendezvous casino. She had black hair, dark brown nipples with very wide aureole, wide hips, chunky butt and thighs. He had noticed her right away because, as she played roulette, leaning over to place her chips on the board, her breasts would almost spill from the top of her dress. There were other, better dressed, slender women who looked better in their clothes, but this one—Lola?—was catching the eyes of all the men around her.

Luckily, it was Clint who caught her eye. They looked at each other across the roulette table, collected their chips and left together. Barely a word passed between them as they made their way to his hotel, undressed each other and spent several very pleasant hours exhausting each other.

She opened her eyes and caught him looking at her.

"Oh God," she said, covering her face. "I was hoping to get out before you saw me in the morning."

"Why would you want to do that, Lola?"

"Why else?" she asked. "So you wouldn't see me in the morning. I'm a fright."

Well, the make-up she had worn was smudged, and her hair was a wild tangle, but what he saw was not a fright.

He leaned over and kissed one of her nipples. Then took it between his teeth. She groaned, dropped her hands from her face to cradle his head as he did the same thing to the other one.

"All I see is a sexy woman who's still in my bed," he said. "And I couldn't be happier about that?"

"Really?" She giggled, reached down between them to find his already hardening cock. "Let's see what I can do about that."

She slithered down between his legs, continued to stoke his hard penis to fullness, and then took it into her mouth and began to suck.

With all the women he had seen the night before, he was dead sure he had made the right choice . . .

***

"Anything else, Mr. Adams?"

He looked up, saw the waitress smiling down at him. He had been replaying the morning in his mind, enjoying it back.

The waitress's name was Alexandra, and she had waited on him every day since he arrived, five days ago. She was a pretty brunette in her early thirties, who very nicely filled out the waitress uniform the hotel made her wear.

"I'll take some more coffee, Alexandra," he said.

She was holding the pot, so she poured immediately. So far, Clint and Alexandra had not seen each other outside of the hotel. That was because, on three consecutive nights, Clint had brought home a different woman from one of the casinos. He was not looking to become more involved than that with anyone on this trip. Lola was the third woman, and he didn't plan to see her again. Luckily, she felt the same way.

"Oh, I read about that lecture," she said, when she saw what he was reading. "Doesn't it sound fascinating?"

"It does," he admitted. He had brought the paper down to breakfast with him to read it again.

"Are you going?" she asked.

"I might."

"Good," she said. "Then maybe I'll see you there, because I'm planning to go. You want this check added to your bill, like the others?"

"Yes, please."

"Waitress!" somebody called, and off she went to take care of her other customers.

Clint stood, folded the newspaper, and carried it outside with him.

***

The position of "concierge" had recently made its way to American hotels from Paris, where it had originated. He was a man who, supposedly, could help a guest with any problem they had. Clint decided to check with him about the lecture, and whether he would need a ticket.

"Why, yes, sir, I believe that is a ticketed event," the fortyish concierge said. "Would you like me to get you one?"

"You can do that?"

The man smiled.

"It's well within my capabilities, sir," the man assured him.

"Good," Clint said. "Then do it. I'll pick it up later."

"I'll leave it at the front desk if I'm not here to hand it to you myself, sir."

"Thanks."

He gave the man a dollar and left the hotel.

***

Clint had gotten himself involved in a poker game that was taking place in a back room at the Alhambra Saloon. It had been a while since he sat in on a poker game with quality players. It had been going before he got there, and would keep going after he left, but for now, he had a chair waiting whenever he walked in.

"'mornin', Mr. Adams," Sam Worthington, the game's host, greeted him at the door. "Ready for your chair?"

"I've got a few hours to kill, Sam," Clint said.

"Then come ahead," Worthington said, "Boys, Clint Adams is comin' back in."

Clint walked to the table, where there was one empty chair among the six.

"Good morning, gents," he said, taking the seat.

"Just in time, Clint," Al Cody said, looking up at him. "Your deal."

Chapter Two

Clint spent several hours playing poker. The chips he had left on the table the day before were brought back, and when he was done for the day, he had twice as many.

Clint waved one of the cashiers over and said, "I'm cashing out for the day."

Not only did the cashier come over, but Worthington came, as well.

"Your chips will be put in the safe until you come back," Worthington assured him.

"Thanks, Sam," Clint said.

He left the poker room and went to the saloon for a beer. The bartender greeted him, having seen him there for the past five days.

"How'd you do?" he asked, setting a beer down.

"I'm still ahead."

"Quittin'?"

"Just for the day."

"When will you cash out for good?"

"I guess when I've had enough."

"So what's on your agenda tonight?" the man asked.

"I'll visit some of the other casinos," Clint said. "Maybe play a little faro, or roulette."

"And back to the table tomorrow?"

"Something new tomorrow," Clint said. "I'm going to a lecture."

"A lecture?" The bartender frowned, but not because he didn't know what a "lecture" was. Clint knew that the man had a college education, and upon graduating had decided to become a bartender. But he was still young enough—in his early thirties—to use his education in the future, if he wanted to. "Where?"

"A museum down on Market street."

"Why?"

"It sounds interesting," Clint said. "It has to do with archeology, something about the Maharajas and Tombs in India."

"Do they play poker there?" the man asked, laughing.

"I'll let you know."

Clint finished his beer and left the Alhambra.

***

To visit some of the higher-class casinos in Portsmouth Square, he had to go back to his hotel to change his clothes. Even the Alhambra would want him to be dressed better if he was going to gamble anywhere but the back room. This was literally the only time the Gunsmith would wear an expensive suit.

As he passed the desk, the desk clerk called out to him.

"Mr. Adams, sir!"

Clint changed course and went to the desk.

"The concierge, Philip, left this for you," the clerk said, handing him an envelope.

"Thank you." He accepted the envelope and went to his room. Once there he opened it and found two tickets for the lecture being held at the San Francisco Museum of Archeological Studies. Obviously, Philip thought he might want to bring a guest.

***

Portsmouth Square was filled with casinos and gambling halls, so many that it would be difficult to visit more than two or three a night, unless you simply walked in, had a drink, and left. If you planned to gamble you were going to be there for a while.

Clint had already spent time over the past few days in the Arcade, the Fontine, the Verandah, the Empire and Lemual Dennison's Exchange.

Tonight his choices were the Parker House, the El Dorado and the Word House.

The hotel he had chosen to stay in was just off the Square, meaning he could easily walk to the casinos he had chosen.

He walked to the Parker House first. As he mounted the steps, several coaches stopped in front to let people out, and he suddenly heard his name.

"Clint Adams, is that you?"

He turned, saw a man who had just stepped from a coach approaching him with a stunning woman on his arm. She was wearing a lavender dress that showed off her toned arms and smooth shoulders.

"Jack?" Clint said. "Jack Gallagher?"

"That's me," Gallagher said, with a smile.

Jack Gallagher was a gambler and a gentleman, probably in that order. In his fifties now, he was tall and barrel-chested, still looked very healthy and prosperous—enough so that he had a much younger woman on his arm.

Gallagher reached for Clint's hand to pump it, but Clint pulled it away after just a few shakes.

"Oh, right," Gallagher said, "your gun hand. Sorry. What brings you to San Francisco?"

"The same as you," Clint said.

"Gambling?" Gallagher asked.

"And the beautiful women."

"Oh, not this one," Gallagher said, quickly. "This is Tania. She's all mine. Honey, meet my friend Clint Adams, the famous Gunsmith."

"It's a pleasure," she said.

Tania was tall, slender, very leggy. She was beautiful, but Gallagher didn't have to worry about competition from Clint. Tania wasn't his type.

Chapter Three

Clint, Gallagher and Tania entered the Parker House together.

"I'm going to start with some faro," Gallagher said. "Honey, you want to come and watch?"

"Do I have to, Jack?" she asked. "Gambling is boring."

"You hear that, Clint?" Gallagher asked. "Gambling is boring."

"I heard."

"Where are you headed, Clint?" Gallagher asked.

"First, to the bar."

"Tania, why don't you go with Clint to the bar? I'm sure he'll buy you a drink."

"Sure," Clint said, "I'd be happy to."

"That suits me," she said, sliding her arm through Clint's left.

"But remember what I said," Gallagher told Clint.

"I know," Clint said. "She's yours."

"Good man!" Gallagher said. "I won't be long. I just need to get a bit ahead before I try roulette."

"Take your time," Tania said, holding Clint's arm tightly. "I'm sure Mr. Adams won't bore me."

"That's Clint, honey," Gallagher said. "Just call him Clint."

"Let's go, Clint," Tania said. "Good luck, Jack."

Gallagher disappeared into the crowd of gamblers, heading for the faro table. Clint and Tania went the other way, to the bar.

When they got to the bar some of the men there made room. Clint didn't have any illusions that it was because of him.

"Step right up, darlin'," one man said to Tania.

"Thank you," she said. "Clint?"

Clint stepped up with her.

"This your fella?" the man asked, stepping closer to Tania but looking at Clint.

"You're wearing a very nice suit," she said to him.

"Well, thank—"

"But you don't have the manners to match it."

"What?" The man looked confused. He had two friends with him, also looking out of place in decent suits. All three were wearing guns.

"I think some of the saloons on the Barbary Coast are missing you and your friends," Tania said.

"What?" he said, again.

"Let me make myself more clear," she said, turning to face him. "You're standing too close."

The man studied her. Clint could see his friends waiting for him to call the play.

"Come on, boys," he said, then. "The women at the Barbary Coast are friendlier, anyway."

The three men left the Parker House.

"What'll you have, folks?" the bow-tied bartender asked.

"Champagne," Tania said, with a smile.

"Make that two," Clint said, thinking he may have been wrong about Tania. Maybe she was his type, after all.

***

Over a couple of glasses of champagne, Clint and Tania got to know each other a little better. She had grown up in Boston, had come West to find excitement. He told her he had come from the East, as well—many, years before.

"You're not that old," she commented.

"Sometimes it just feels that way," he told her.

"How do you know Jack?" she asked.

"I sat across from him at some poker tables over the years," he said.

"So you're a gambler, and a gunfighter?"

"Who said I was a gunfighter?"

"I just thought—I mean, your reputation . . . did I just insult you? If I did, I'm sorry."

"Forget it," Clint said. "Here comes your escort, now."

Gallagher joined them at the bar.

"Well," he said, "that was profitable, just as I thought it would be."

"You mean, just as you hoped, don't you?" Tania asked.

"No," he said, "just like I knew it would be. You ready to play some roulette?"

"I guess so," she said. "It's the only gambling I don't find boring."

"That's because that little white ball goes around and round every few minutes, or so," Gallagher said. "Clint?"

"You go ahead," Clint said. "I might try some blackjack."

"I heard there's a backroom poker game going on somewhere," Gallagher said. "Would you know anything about that?"

"I might."

"Then we should have a drink and talk later," Gallagher said.

"I'll count on it," Clint said.

As Gallagher walked away with the stunning Tania on his arm, the bartender asked, "You just lose your girl?"

"Naw," Clint said, "she came in with him. I was just minding her for a bit."

"You want another glass of champagne, then?"

"No," Clint said, "bring me a cold beer."

Chapter Four

Clint killed some time playing blackjack, lost a few dollars because he didn't have the patience. It just wasn't a game he liked as much as poker.

He walked away from the blackjack table and over to one of the roulette wheels, where the white ball was dancing around the spinning wheel while hopeful eyes looked on. Some of the gambler's heads were even bobbing up and down as they actually tried to follow the ball, rather than just waiting for it to settle.

As the ball came to a stop, followed by the wheel, and a woman whooped, he realized it was Tania.

"I told you this is the only game that's not boring!" she cried out.

She waited for the croupier to stack her chips, and then raked them in happily. Clint saw Gallagher lean over and say something to her, to which she shook her head and started placing chips on numbers. She was playing so many numbers, that a hit might not even make her a profit.

She didn't seem to care. Hitting a number was her only concern.

Clint caught Gallagher's eye and gestured to him. The gambler said something to Tania, who barely nodded as she kept her eyes on the board.

"She likes hitting her number," Clint commented.

"Yeah, the only problem is, they're almost all her numbers."

"I'm going to move on to another house," Clint said. "You asked about that back room poker game? It's over at the Alhambra. Ask for Sam Worthington."

"Who's playing?"

"Al Cody's there, but he's the only gambler I've seen. The others have money, but no talent."

"Cody, huh? I'll give it some thought. We won't be here much longer. Thanks. Maybe I'll see you there."

Gallagher went back to Tania, who was whooping again as she raked in chips.

As Clint turned to leave he saw something that slowed him down . . .

***

When Jack Gallagher and Tania left the Parker House, two men also stepped out the door right behind them. Their carriage was waiting out front for them, and as Gallagher opened the door for Tania, the two men quickened their pace. As they reached Gallagher, who was about to assist Tania into the carriage, they shoved their guns into his back.

"The little lady was doin' pretty good in there," one of them said.

"Let's see the money," the second one ordered.

"My friends," Gallagher said, "she hit plenty of numbers, but she didn't make a cent."

"Don't kid us," the first man said, "we saw her rakin' in those chips."

"I know you did, but I'm tellin' you—"

The first man dug the gun deeper into Gallagher's back.

"Jack," Tania said, "make these two bores go away."

"Bores, huh?" the second man said. He took his gun out of Gallagher's back and moved closer to Tania. "Lemme show ya who's a bore, lady."

He grabbed for her purse. She pulled it away, and then swung it and hit him on the shoulder with it.

"Get away from us!" she snapped.

"Tania—" Gallagher said, but he stopped when he heard the hammer click back on the gun behind him.

Then, suddenly, the gun was gone and a heavy weight slammed into him as the man fell to the ground. Gallagher staggered, but kept his balance.

"What the—" he said.

"Hey, Rich," the second man said, then looked at something behind Gallagher.

"Put the gun away, friend," Clint said, "and help your friend up. Then both of you do what the lady said and get going."

Gallagher turned, saw Clint standing there with his gun still in his holster.

"Mister," the second man said, "are you crazy?"

"No," Gallagher said, "he's not crazy, he's the Gunsmith."

"What?"

"Go ahead," Tania yelled, "shoot 'im, Clint!"

"Now, w-wait a minute—" the man stammered, quickly holstering his weapon. "See? I'm helpin' him up and we're goin'."

"Go faster," Clint said.

"Yessir!"

He pulled his friend to his feet and yanked him along as fast as he could, off into the darkness.

"Thanks for that," Gallagher said to Clint.

"I saw them eyeing you inside," Clint said. "They heard Tania shouting about her wins."

"You should've shot them," she said.

"Then I'd have a lot of explaining to do to the law," Clint said, "and I've still got some gambling to do tonight. I'll say good-night to you both. Tania, I'd keep a little quiet about my victories, if I was you."

"It's boring to keep quiet," she said. "This was exciting."

Gallagher looked at Clint and shrugged.

Chapter Five

Clint went to the Word House next, hoping he wouldn't encounter Gallagher and Tania again. He didn't. But he wondered if Gallagher would be able to get away from her in order to join the back-room game at the Alhambra. It would be nice to have another talented poker player in that game other than Al Cody.

After a beer and a few hands of faro at the Word House, Clint moved on to Sam McCabe and Thomas Chambers' El Dorado. He knew McCabe, but not the other owner, but it didn't matter. Neither of them were in view, as he entered.

The El Dorado had one of the longest bars Clint had ever seen, and still he had to elbow himself some room in order to get a beer. The air was filled with the sound of chips hitting chips as they were tossed onto the table, or simply being played with, and he could hear the sound of that little white ball at the roulette tables. He listened for Tania's whooping, but it never came.

He didn't feel like blackjack or faro there, so he simply turned his back to the bar and sipped his beer as he watched some of the action. Several pretty ladies went by and gave him a look, but they were on the arm of another man, so he did nothing suggestive in return.

It was unusual to see unescorted ladies in these casinos. Clint had found two over the past three nights, and brought them back to his hotel. The third woman he dallied with was a girl who worked at the Empire—not as a saloon girl, but a hostess.

Tonight he wasn't seeing any likely ladies to spend time with, so he resolved to have a second beer and then go back to his hotel. After all, he had the lecture the next day. It was taking place pretty early, so he wanted to come down with enough time to have breakfast first.

As Clint was leaving the El Dorado, he heard off in the shadows, what definitely sounded like a fight. He considered minding his business, but instead he headed that way to see if he was right.

There was an alley between The El Dorado and the next building, and that was where the noise was coming from. Clint peered into the alley, which was lit by a shaft of moonlight. He saw a lone man, at that moment, surrounded by four men with whom he was fighting. They were circling him, and from the looks of all of them, plenty of blows had already been exchanged.

The lone man in the center was a tall and fit gent, and as Clint approached, he could see his face in the moonlight. He looked unconcerned about the situation and, if anything, almost as if he was enjoying himself, despite the fact that his clothes were torn.

The four men closed on him again, and the man moved quickly, putting two of them on their butts with a single blow each, and then addressing the other two.

Clint didn't see any weapons, so he decided to just watch a while longer, since the lone man didn't seem to need any help.

The man absorbed some blows and shook them off, then returned them with gusto. Before long, all four of his attackers were on their asses, wondering what had happened.

"You need any help?" Clint called out.

The man looked over at him and actually smiled.

"No, no, that's okay," he said, "I've got this. These four thought I was easy pickings. Their mistake."

One of the men looked at Clint, then said to his compadres, "Let's get out of here."

They all got to their feet and ran past Clint, who could see that there wasn't a gun among them. Then he looked at the lone man in the torn clothes, who also didn't have a gun.

"You okay?" Clint asked.

The man looked down at himself.

"It looks worse than it is," he said. "But thanks for asking." The man approached him. Clint could see he was in his thirties, and very fit. "I'd buy you a drink, but I think I just better get back to my hotel and change."

"I understand," Clint said.

"I'm at the Bella Union," the man said. "My name's Smith."

"Really?"

The man shrugged.

"Hey," he said, "somebody's got to be named Smith, right?"

"I suppose so," Clint said. "I'm Clint Adams."

The name didn't seem to mean anything to the man, and that was okay.

They shook hands and the man said, "Come by the Union sometime and I'll buy you a drink."

"I'll remember, Mr. Smith."

The man waved and went walking off, not even a limp in his step after battling four attackers on his own.

Clint turned and walked in the opposite direction, back to his hotel.

***

"Mr. Adams!" the clerk called. It was the same man who had given him the tickets from the concierge. Clint walked over to the desk.

"What is it?"

"Sir, a lady came in looking for you."

"And?"

"She wanted me to let her into your room."

"And did you?"

"No, sir," he said.

"So where is she?"

"She became angry and left," the man said. "I'm sorry if I did wrong, but—"

"No, no," Clint said. "You did exactly right. I don't want you letting anybody into my room."

The man seemed relieved.

"Did she leave a message?"

"Nossir," the clerk said. "She stormed out."

Clint thought about asking the clerk what she looked like, but decided against it. He doubted it had been any of the women he had already been with. They all seemed to have the same attitude he did, that once was enough. Whoever it was could always come back and try again, when he was there.

"Okay," Clint said. "Thank you."

As Clint started away the clerk asked, "Uh, sir?"

"Yes?"

"What do I do if she comes back?"

"If I'm in my room," Clint said, "let her come up."

"And if not?"

"The same thing you did tonight," Clint said. "Just make her mad."

Chapter Six

Because the clerk had told him he hadn't allowed the woman into his room, Clint simply unlocked his door and entered. As soon as he felt the presence of someone there, he drew his gun and went into a crouch.

"Whoa! Hold on!" Tania said. "Don't shoot."

"How'd you get in here?" Clint asked. "The clerk told me he turned a woman away."

"He did," Tania said. "Don't blame him. I came up the back way and let myself in."

"How'd you get the door open?"

Seated on the edge of the bed, still wearing the same gown from earlier that evening, she smiled and said, "It's one of my hidden talents."

Clint holstered his gun, but still didn't close the door. "Where's Jack?"

She shrugged.

"Drinking, gambling," she said, "somewhere."

"You're not worried he'll miss you?"

"I told him I was going to bed," she said, patting the mattress. "I meant it."

"Now wait—"

"I've waited long enough," she said. "Close the door, Clint. And don't tell me you don't want me. Jack and me, we're not married. We're not even a couple. In fact, we met today and ain't never been to bed. So you're not stealin' another man's woman."

"Still," Clint said, "Jack did meet you first."

"But he never impressed me," she said. "You have, more than once."

"I have to admit," he said, "you've impressed me, too, and I don't mean just with your beauty."

"I'm not beautiful," she said, "but I know what you mean. I tend to speak my mind."

"What makes you say you're not beautiful?" he asked.

"I can look in a mirror," she said. "My nose is too small, my eyes are too wide apart—"

"Stop picking at yourself," he said. "Look at the whole package. You're a stunner."

"Well, there you go," she said, standing up, "now you're talkin' like a man who's interested."

"I never said I wasn't interested."

"Good," she said, "then I won't be embarrassed when I do this."

She reached behind her, undid her gown and let it drop to the floor. Underneath she wore nothing. She had high, hard breasts with rosy nipples, very clear, smooth skin and long, graceful legs. Between her legs was a bush of hair that matched the auburn mass on her lovely head.

"Well," he said, "now you've impressed me again."

He went to her and took her into his arms . . .

***

. . . and she continued to impress him.

After some feverish kisses, they gravitated to the bed, where he paused to hang his gunbelt and undress, before joining her. When they pressed their bodies together, her skin was burning and his hard penis was trapped between them.

"Oh my," she said, reaching down, "talk about impressive . . ."

"Let's stop talking," he said, and silenced her with yet another long, hot kiss. She didn't argue.

Abruptly, she pushed him down onto his back with surprising strength, then slid down so that she was between his legs. She stroked his cock for a while, then wet it thoroughly with her tongue before taking it into her hot mouth. She took her time, seeming to really want to enjoy it, so he didn't object. He settled back with his hands behind his head.

He watched as her head bobbed up and down, enjoyed the feel of her lips on his shaft, her tongue on the spongy head, and her hands massaging his testicles. She worked him right up to the point of bursting, then backed off, releasing him from her mouth, tightening her fingers around the base of his shaft.

"Jesus," he said, gasping for breath.

"I know," she said, smiling up at him with bright, shiny violet eyes, "not bad, huh?"

"Get up here," he snapped, grabbing for her. He got his hands under her arms and pulled her up. She landed on top of him, pinning his cock beneath her, and lifted her hips, thinking he wanted to enter her. Instead, he flipped her onto her back, slid down between her long legs, and started returning the favor.

He used his lips and tongue, and his fingers, to work her pussy to the point of gushing, wetting his face and the sheet beneath them. Then he moved up so that he was hovering above her. He pressed the head of his hard cock to her wet pussy lips and slid into her with ease. He went in slowly, though, wanting to draw it out rather than ram it into her hard.

"Oooh," she groaned, as he inched into her. "That's soooo nice."

"Hang on," he told her, "it's going to get nicer."

***

They spent most of their time trying to impress each other even more. But in the end they drifted off to sleep, locked together, legs entwined, with her sleeping on his left shoulder by his design, so as to keep his gun arm free.

Well before morning, Tania stirred and sat up in bed.

"I've got to go," she said, swinging her legs to the floor.

"Why?" he asked.

She looked at him over her shoulder and said, "You don't want to know."

"What's that mean?"

She reached for her gown, grabbed it off the floor, stood up and started to slip into it.

"Jack will be looking for me," she said.

"I thought you said you two weren't—"

She turned to face him, straightening her gown.

"I said what I had to say to get you into bed," she told him.

He sat up.

"And why doesn't that surprise me?"

"I'm not going to apologize," she said. "I think we both enjoyed it."

"You're right about that."

"But it can't happen again."

"You're right about that, too."

"Oh yeah," she said, putting her hands on her hips, "if I came back, you'd turn me away."

"I would."

She stared at him.

"You know, I think you would."

"Good night, Tania."

"What? No good night kiss?"

"Say hi to Jack for me."

"I don't think so," she said. "He might call off our wedding."

"Get out!"

Chapter Seven

Nobody knocked on his door that night, which suited him just fine. He had a good night's sleep after Tania left and woke early enough to go downstairs and have a leisurely breakfast before heading over to the museum.

He carried both tickets with him, even though he had no idea who he'd give the second one to. He might have invited a lady, but he didn't know any that this sort of thing would appeal to. In the end he decided this was something he should do alone.

When he reached the museum he was surprised to find quite a few people ascending the stairs in front and behind him. This professor of archeology seemed to be attracting quite a crowd for his lecture. And since Clint had never been to one before, he didn't know if this was something crowds of people normally attended.

Inside the museum they were all directed to an auditorium, where many of the seats had already been occupied. Clint decided to sit in the last row, with his back against the wall, and on the aisle, so that he only had one person sitting next to him. The auditorium was not as large as some theaters he had been in, and he was sure he would be able to see what was happening on stage quite well.

At the moment, the only thing that was on the stage was a podium the speaker would stand at.

There were some young people—boys and girls—at the doors, handing out programs. Clint had accepted one, and now he leafed through it. There was information on some digs the speaker had been on already in India, one of which had apparently unearthed a four-thousand-year-old tomb. Clint found that fascinating, since the history of the United States only went back one hundred and ten years or so.

He did not find it odd that the speaker's name was Professor Henry Smith, since Smith was a fairly common name. He had just met a man named Smith the night before. There were some photos of tombs and mummies and such in the program, but none of the speaker.

As a man ascended to the stage and walked to the podium, he lowered the program and paid attention. As it turned out, all the seats in the auditorium were not taken, so he had several empty seats to his right, and two empty ones in front of him. Most of the people in attendance preferred to sit up closer, which suited him.

"Ladies and gentlemen," the roly-poly man said, "my name is Alexander Siverling, and I am the Curator of this wonderful museum."

There was a smattering of applause.

"I want to welcome all to this very informative lecture by one of the leading archeologists in this country. He's going to describe for us some of the many adventures he has had, and some that he still intends to have. Without any further delay, I introduce to you Professor Henry Smith."

The speaker rose from where he was seated in the first row, and ascended to the stage. At the podium he shook hands with the curator, who then stepped off the stage and sat down in the first row.

The speaker waited for the applause to die down before beginning.

The nearest person to Clint was a young girl sitting in the row in front of him, several seats down. Still, she turned to look at him and ask, "Isn't he just so handsome?"

"Yes," Clint agreed, "very."

The speaker was not only handsome, but very fit. The very attributes Clint had noticed the night before when he had seen Professor Smith in the alley next to the El Dorado. Battling with four thugs, the man had enjoyed every minute of it.

And now he was on stage, getting ready to give a lecture.

The same Smith.

Maybe it wasn't so common a name, after all.

Chapter Eight

Professor Henry Smith was apparently as good a speaker as he was a fighter. He held that crowd in the palm of his hand with his stories of adventures past.

And then he started talking the future.

". . . and now," he said, "I am about to go back to India for a wonderful new find. I'll be leaving very soon, and I am accepting contributions to put together my war chest. You see, these trips are not cheap and must be financed by . . . well, let's call them investors. Of course, the museum is kind enough to fund some of it, but . . . well, as I was saying, the job involves one of the very oldest Maharajas, and his tomb . . ."

Clint was surprised the professor was asking for money, but he also knew the man was at least competent in two areas: fighting and talking. So it was likely he was also a competent archeologist.

After he finished his lecture—and appeal for funds—he got plenty of applause. People lined up to talk to him afterward. Clint decided to just stand in line and wait his turn.

When he reached the front of the line he said, "One of us owes the other a drink, but I forgot which is which."

Professor Smith looked at Clint, and his smile lit up his face.

"Clint Adams, right?"

"Right."

"I am so glad you came," Smith said. "Did I tell you about this?"

"No, I read about it in the newspaper," Clint said. "When we met last night, I had no idea this would be you."

"Coincidence, huh?"

"I hate that word, but yeah, that's what it looks like."

"I tell you what," Smith said. "Let me finish up here and we'll go get that drink. Give me . . . fifteen minutes."

"I'll wait outside."

Clint turned and headed for the door. He was surprised to see how many people in line were holding either cash or a check in their hands, anxious to give their money away. And many of them were women, including the girl who had been sitting in the row in front of Clint.

She smiled as he went by and asked, "Is he as handsome up close?"

"Even more," he said, and went outside to wait.

***

Clint sat on the museum steps, watching people come and go. After about twenty minutes Professor Smith came out of the building and walked down the steps.

"Sorry I'm late," he said. "I'm glad you waited."

"I've got nothing better to do," Clint said.

"Well, now you do," Smith said. "Let's go get a drink. There's a place around the corner."

Clint had worn one of the suits he'd bought for the casinos, but no vest or tie. Smith was wearing a clean shirt and trousers, but no jacket—and the man didn't carry a gun.

"Lead the way," Clint said.

They went down the stairs and started around the corner.

"There was a young lady sitting in front of me who was very impressed with you," Clint said.

"Cute?"

"Very."

"Money?"

"No."

"Too bad."

"So is this what you usually do before a trip?" Clint asked. "Beg for money?"

"I'm not begging for money," Smith said. "I'm soliciting investors. There's a difference."

"How much do you get from the museum?"

"Very little."

"But you said—"

"I want people to think I'm being funded," Smith said. "Sometimes I say it's a university. Truth is, the museum allowed me to lecture because I said I'd do it for free."

"So you could beg—"

Smith raised a finger.

"—sorry, solicit funding."

"Right."

Clint put his hand on the man's arm and they stopped walking.

"Is this on the level?"

"The trip? Absolutely. Mummy, tomb, Maharaja, the whole thing. Hey, you want to come?"

"How much would it cost me?" Clint asked.

"Nothing," Smith said. "I'm not trying to get money from you. I just think I could use you."

"For what?"

"Protection."

"Against what?"

"Were you listening back there?"

"To most of it."

"Let's go get that drink," Smith said, "and I'll explain."

Chapter Nine

Around the corner was a small saloon called PADDY O'DOYLE'S PUB. Clint only knew what a "pub" was because he had been to London, England a long time ago. This one was obviously Irish.

They got two beers from a barman with a heavy Irish accent and took them to a back table. That early in the day, the place was mostly empty, except for a few regulars.

"This next trip to India could be the biggest ever," Smith told Clint. "There's only one drawback."

"And what's that?"

"It's nothing, really" Smith said. "I mean, nothing so big . . . not really . . ."

"What are we talking about, Professor?" Clint asked.

"It's just . . . a curse."

"A what?"

"It's called a Maharaja's Curse," Smith said. "There were often curses put on Maharaja's tombs to keep people from breaking in, and . . ."

"And what?"

"Well," he said, "to keep the Maharaja from breaking out."

"The dead man?"

"The mummy, yeah."

"They break out?"

"That's what the people in India believe," Smith said. "And even some people in the United States."

"Like who?"

"Like people who spend time in museums."

"People who believe in curses?"

"Among other things."

"Or are you just trying to get me to go by telling me something you think I'll find interesting?" Clint asked. "The same thing you do with people when you're asking them to, uh, invest."

Smith shook his head.

"Everything I say about my trip to India is on the level," he insisted.

"And you want me to go with you."

"Sure, why not?"

"As protection."

"Well," Smith said, "to tell you the truth, whether you come with me or not, I may need your help to get me on the boat—alive."

"Okay," Clint said, "now I'm interested. Tell me more."

***

"Somebody is trying to stop me from going," Smith told Clint, as they moved on to a second beer.

"Stopping you how?"

"Well," he said, "last night they were trying to injure me, maybe kill me."

"And that's happened before?"

"Twice," Smith said. "Once before three men started a fight. It happened as I was on my way here to San Francisco. They actually tried to toss me off the moving train."

"And what happened?"

"I managed to fight them off, and throw one of them off," Smith said.

"And the other time?"

"A coach almost ran me down on the street after I got here," the Professor said.

"I've got to say," Clint said, "you seem to be pretty good at fighting these attempts off by yourself."

"Yes," Smith said, "until somebody tries to kill me with a gun."

"Why don't you carry one?"

"I'm pretty handy with my fists," Smith said. "I was on the boxing team in college. And I can handle a whip, and a sword. But I'm only average with a gun. I think once, whoever it is, decides to just shoot me down and get it over with, that's when I'm going to need expert help."

"And who would you have gone to if we hadn't met?" Clint asked.

"I have no idea," Smith said. "I suppose I would've hired a bodyguard, maybe a Pinkerton."

"Pinkertons are pretty good at some things," Clint said, "like strike breaking. But as bodyguards?"

"See?" Smith said. "I need you. We were supposed to meet."

"But you said something about a curse."

"The curse hasn't reared its ugly head, yet," Smith told him.

"Yet?" Clint asked. "You believe in the curse?"

"Look," Smith said, "I've seen a lot of things I can't explain in my travels. A curse wouldn't even be the most unbelievable. But wouldn't a trip to India be something new for you?"

"Brand new," Clint admitted.

"And you wouldn't have to pay a nickel for it," Smith added.

"Providing you get the investors you're looking for," Clint said.

"Well, yeah . . . but I will."

Clint studied Professor Henry Smith. Was the man waiting for him to offer some money? Was this all a scam to get Clint to invest?

"Okay, look," Clint said, "let's see if you get the money you're after, and then we'll talk about me going along."

"And what about being my bodyguard?" Smith asked. "If you decide not to go to India with me, I'll pay you for your time."

"We'll talk about money later," Clint said. "For now let's say I'm your bodyguard."

"Excellent!"

"The first thing you have to do is change hotels."

"But I like the Bella Union."

"And people know you're staying there," Clint pointed out.

"What do you suggest?"

"I want you to move to my hotel, The Palladium," Clint said. "It's just outside of Portsmouth Square."

"I can do that," Smith said.

"Now," Clint said. "I want you to do it now. Let's go over there and check you out."

They paid for their beers and left the pub.

"Do you have any other lectures scheduled?" Clint asked, on the street.

"Oh yes," Smith said. "I've only started my investment drive."

"Okay," Clint said, "I'll need a list."

Chapter Ten

Clint stood at the door of Henry Smith's room while the Professor packed his bags.

"You're serious about this bodyguarding business," Smith observed.

"That's what you want, isn't it?" Clint asked.

"Well, yes," Smith said, "especially after last night."

"I just thought they were trying to rob you," Clint told him.

"So did I, until they made it clear they knew who I was," Smith said.

"Ah," Clint said, "that would do it. Do you have a list of the rest of your, uh . . ."

". . . investment meetings?"

"Right."

Smith crossed the room, grabbed a piece of paper, handed it to Clint, and then went back to his packing, He had two large suitcases, and a large trunk.

While he finished packing, Clint looked at the list. There were five dates and places on it, all in the San Francisco area. They were all scheduled at hotels—none of which were in Portsmouth Square.

"Why not do it in any of the Portsmouth Square hotels?" Clint asked.

"I thought about it, but I don't think gamblers would be interested in anything but gambling."

"You're probably right about that," Clint agreed.

Smith finished the two suitcases and walked to the trunk. He didn't open it, just locked it up.

"What's in there?"

"A lot of my equipment that I'll be using once we get to India—my clothes, my hat, my whip, my gun—"

"Why not wear the gun now?"

"Because if I have to get it out real quick, I'll probably shoot myself in the foot," Smith said. "No, now that I've got you, I'll leave the gun there until we get to Delhi."

"Well," Clint said, "we'll need somebody to carry it down—"

"Not at all," Smith said. "If you take those two, I can manage the trunk."

With that he leaned over, grabbed the trunk with one hand and hiked it up onto his shoulder. He was obviously a very powerful man.

Clint picked up the two suitcases from the bed and they left the room to head down to the lobby.

***

Downstairs they set the luggage by the desk and Smith checked out.

"Professor, we thought you'd be with us another week or so," the clerk said.

"Something came up," Smith said, signing his bill. "But thanks for the hospitality."

They picked up the bags again and carried them to the front door.

"I didn't see any cash change hands there," Clint said.

"That's because they were donating the room to my cause," Smith replied.

Smith waved to the doorman and told him they needed a cab.

"I don't know about the Palladium going for that," Clint said, while they waited.

"I guess we'll have to see," Smith said. "I'll talk to the manager when we get there. I just might be able to convince him."

"Well," Clint said, "I guess if anyone is able to convince them to give you a free room, it's you."

"And," Professor Smith said, "I might be able to get one for you, too."

Chapter Eleven

When they got to the Palladium, a doorman helped them bring the luggage in to the front desk, and from there Clint left it all up to Professor Henry Smith. He asked for and got an audience with the manager of the hotel in his office while Clint waited in the lobby.

When he came back out, the manager was with him.

"Eric," the natty little man said to the desk clerk, "have these bags brought up to Professor Smith's room."

"Yessir."

"Mr. Lincoln," Smith said to the manager, "this is Clint Adams."

"Mr. Adams," the manager said, shaking Clint's hand, "I had no idea you were in my hotel. Would you like to be moved to a better room?"

"No, sir, the room I have is just fine," Clint assured him.

"Why didn't you ask for me when you checked in?"

"Well, sir, I like to keep a low profile," Clint said. "I'd appreciate it if this didn't get around."

"Of course not," Lincoln said. "We're nothing if not discreet. But I want to assure you that your room and Professor Smith's room will be on the house."

"I appreciate that, sir," Clint said.

Lincoln turned to Smith.

"Professor, if you need anything else, just let the clerk know and he'll get it for you. And if he can't, I will."

"I'll do that, sir. Thank you."

Two uniformed bellmen came running over and grabbed the suitcases. Two more came and hefted the trunk, and they all walked up the stairs to the second floor.

Smith got a room right down the hall from Clint. Inside Clint walked to the window, looked and saw with satisfaction that there was no access from the street below.

"Just stay away from the window," Clint said. "We don't want anyone taking a shot from a rooftop across the way."

"Don't worry," Smith said. "I've got no reason to be looking out the window."

He tipped the four bellmen, who thanked him and left.

"That's the thing about a free room," he told Clint. "It leaves you free to tip well."

"What are your plans now?" Clint asked.

"Right now," Smith said. "I'm thinking about lunch."

"Exactly what I was thinking," Clint said. "They have a good dining room here."

"Lead the way."

***

As they entered the dining room, Alexandra spotted Clint and waved him over to a table.

"Alexandra, this is my friend, Professor Henry Smith."

"Oh, my God," she said, pointing. "You're Henry Smith!"

"I just said that," Clint replied.

"No, you don't understand," she said. "He's been to Egypt." She pointed at Smith. "You've been to Egypt."

"I have."

"You've discovered mummies."

"Yes, I have," Smith said.

"Alexandra," Clint said, "how do you know all this?"

"I read the papers," she said, "and I read his book."

"Book?"

"You read that?" Smith asked. "I didn't think anybody ever read it." He looked at Clint. "I wrote it a few years ago, about a dig in India."

"You're amazing!" Alexandra said.

"And hungry," Clint said.

"Oh, right," she said. "Lunch?"

"Definitely," Smith said.

"What would you like?" she asked.

The two men sat and Smith said, "Why don't you bring me whatever you recommend."

"And you?" she asked Clint.

"I'll have the same," Clint said.

"Comin' up," she said. "Coffee?"

"Yes," Smith said.

"Two," Clint said.

She looked at Smith and said, "Henry Smith."

He smiled at her.

"You're much more handsome in person."

"Thank you," he said, "you're not so bad yourself."

She blushed, and hurried to the kitchen, ignoring several tables who reached out to her.

"Pretty woman," Smith said.

"Yes, she is. And she's impressed by you."

"That happens sometimes," Smith said. "People only think about the flashy, exciting part of what I do."

"There's more?"

"There's days, weeks, months digging in the dirt," Smith said. "Nothing flashy about that."

"How'd you get interested in it?"

"My father was an archeologist," Smith said. "Used to take me on digs with him."

"To Egypt?"

"Among other places," Smith said.

"India?"

"No," Smith said. "That'll be new for me. He went but never took me."

"Where is he now?"

"He died, years ago," Smith said. He leaned forward, his elbows on the table. "You want to know what he died of?"

"Sure."

"A curse."

"Come on."

"That's what my mother said," Smith went on. "It was a Maharaja's curse that killed my father."

"And that cinched it for you, huh?"

"Oh yeah," Smith said. "I decided in college that I was going to find the curse that killed my dad."

"And have you?"

"No," Smith said, "not yet."

"But you're still looking?"

"All the time." Smith sat back. "Every dig, I'm hopeful. I find Kings, Maharajas, Maharinis and tombs, and every time I'm hopeful I'm going to learn more about it."

"What if it wasn't a curse?"

"I'm trying to find that out, too."

"So you do," Clint asked, "or you don't believe in a Maharaja's curse?"

Smith shook his head and said, "I'm just not sure."

Chapter Twelve

Alexandra brought out steaming bowls of beef stew, which she assured them was the specialty of the house.

"Why didn't you ever tell me that?" Clint asked.

"Because," she told him, "you always order steak."

"It's delicious," Smith told her. "Thank you."

"You're very welcome."

As she walked away, Smith said, "She likes you."

"Me?" Clint asked. "She's paying attention to you."

"She's just trying to make you jealous."

"I don't think so," Clint said. "I think she's taken with you."

"Then it's too bad I don't have time for romance," Smith said. "But if I did, I like my women a little more . . . exotic."

"And dead?" Clint asked. "Wrapped in bandages?"

Smith laughed.

"Now you're getting the idea."

***

"When Smith asked Alexandra what he owed her, she said, "Oh, we got the word from Mr. Lincoln. You get anything you want." She stared right into his eyes. "Anything."

"This is for you," he said, handing her some money.

"Thank you, Professor." She tucked the cash into the pocket of her apron and left.

"See what I mean about free things?" Smith said to Clint. "She just got a nice big tip."

"That's only going to make her like you more, Professor," Clint said.

"Oh."

"If she knocks on your door tonight," Clint said, "make sure it's her before you open it."

Back in the lobby Clint asked, "Where to now?"

"Upstairs," Smith said. "I've got to dress for my next pitch."

"Tonight?"

"Didn't you read the list I gave you?"

"I skimmed it."

"I need to change into something more . . ." he gave it a second, ". . . adventurous."

"Okay, then, let's go." As they walked across the lobby, Clint asked, "Do I need to change?"

"Nope," Smith said, shaking his head. "Just make sure you keep your gun on."

"I always have my gun," Clint said.

"Really? Even in the bath?"

"It's nearby."

"And when you're with a woman?"

"Hanging on the bedpost."

"Wow," Smith said as they went up the stairs, "what a tough way to live."

"And when you're in India on a dig, aren't you always on the lookout for trouble?"

"Well, yeah, but—"

"That's my life," Clint said. "Like I'm always on a dig."

"But not as dirty, I'll bet."

"Dirty enough."

They walked down the hall to Smith's room. He stopped at the door.

"Are you going to come in and watch me change?"

"No," Clint said, "but I'll watch your door."

"Good enough."

Smith went inside. Clint walked to his own room, went inside, but his door was ajar so he could see Smith's door. Nothing happened for twenty minutes, and then Smith came back out. He was wearing a shirt and trousers of a material that would be perfect for the desert, as well as a hat Clint had heard called "A bush hat."

"Quite a costume," Clint said, stepping out of his room.

"There you are. Well, you know, sometimes you've got to look the part."

"And this is how people expect you to look when you go mummy hunting?"

"Exactly."

"So where to?"

"There's a university across town that's waiting to give me money," Smith said. "All I've got to do is convince them."

"Well," Clint said, "this should be interesting."

***

The doorman got them a cab, which they took to the university building. This time the auditorium was crowded. Clint still insisted on sitting in the last row, his back to the wall, and told Smith he would see him afterward.

"What if something happens?" Smith asked. "What are you going to do from back there?"

"So where do you want me?"

"Up front, where I can see you."

"Okay," Clint said, pointing to the right, "I'll be against that wall."

"Fine," Smith said. "I'll see you after."

Clint took his place and, after an introduction that made him sound like some sort of holy man, Professor Henry Smith stepped to the podium to make his pitch.

Chapter Thirteen

"How'd you do?" Clint asked, as they left the building.

"Not bad," Smith said, "but I've still got a long way to go."

"Do you expect to make the money you need off that list you showed me?"

"I hope so."

"And if not?"

Smith shrugged.

"Then I'll make a new list."

They caught a cab in front of the building and headed back to the hotel.

"What's next?" Clint asked, along the way.

"I was thinking about what you said concerning Portsmouth Square," Smith said. "Maybe I should visit some of the casinos, talk to some of the gamblers. Who knows? There might be a few Maharaja enthusiasts there."

"You never know," Clint agreed.

"Will you take me on a tour?"

"I'll show you a few places."

"Introduce me to some people?"

"I know a few."

"Then let me change out of this get-up, and we'll start.

"Get-up? Isn't that actually what you wear on your digs?" Clint asked.

"It is," Smith said, "but here in America, it's a get-up."

***

Clint followed Smith's example and changed into something more fitting of Portsmouth Square in the daytime. He wore a suit but, once again, no vest or tie. He was presentable, but not "dressed to the nines."

He met Smith in the lobby, again. The man looked fine enough for a daytime casino romp.

"So tell me," Clint said, as they left the hotel, "anybody knock on your door last night?"

"You mean Alexandra?" Smith asked. "No such luck. I slept all night, all by myself."

"Too bad," Clint said. "She's a nice woman, and she's impressed by you."

"And you?"

"She didn't knock on my door, either," Clint assured him.

"Then it'll be interesting to see which one she chooses," Smith said, laughing. "Do we need a cab?"

"No, we're going to walk," Clint said. "We'll hit the Verandah, the Empire and the Arcade. They're very active, no matter what the hour."

"Good," Smith said, "and I've got cash I can use to buy drinks."

"That'll help," Clint said. "Just don't ask for money right out. They'll only think you want to gamble it."

"I've got that figured," Smith said. "My plan is to let people invest, not ask them to."

"That sounds like a good plan."

***

As impressed as Clint was with Smith's pitch while standing up in front of an audience of expectant people, he was even more impressed with the Professor's demeanor at a bar.

Within five minutes of entering the Verandah, Smith had a crowd of people around him at the bar, listening to his stories of mummies and tombs of Maharajas.

"What is a Maharaja, anyway," a pretty woman asked.

"A Maharaja," Smith explained, "is like a king."

"And they buried their kings in these tombs?" she asked.

"Yes," he said. "It was their way of paying homage to them."

"And you," another woman said, "go over there and dig them up?"

"That's right."

"How exciting!"

All he had to do was get them worked up about the adventure so they would want to be part of it. And most of the people he was talking to were the other half of couples where one gambled, and one just stood at the bar and waited. This gave those bar flies something to think about.

Like investing . . .

***

Their visits to the Arcade and the Empire went pretty much the same way. Clint didn't stand around the bar with Smith. He walked around, made some plays at the roulette wheel or faro table, came back and joined the Professor later on.

His third time around at the Empire, he actually found Smith standing alone.

"Where did your fans go?" Clint asked.

"They had to move on," Smith said, "but I think I made some very good contacts, Clint. How about a beer with me to celebrate? I'm buying."

"I thought you'd never ask."

Chapter Fourteen

They made one more stop.

Clint decided to take Smith to the Alhambra Hotel and casino. It would give him a chance to check on the progress of the poker game.

"This is even livelier," Smith said, as they entered.

"There's a lot going on," Clint said. "Go ahead and tell your stories. I want to check on something in one of the back rooms."

"Okay," Smith said, "I'll see you at the bar."

Clint left Smith and went to knock on the back-room door. Sam Worthington answered.

"I wondered where you were," he said, letting Clint enter.

"I got involved in something else," Clint said, "but I think I sent you a replacement."

"Oh, you mean Gallagher? Yeah, he's here, and he's cleanin' up."

"What about Cody?"

"Holdin' his own," Worthington said. "When are you comin' back in?"

"I'll let you know," Clint said.

"What are you involved in that's so important?" Worthington asked.

Clint saw the interest in the man's eyes.

"Just an investment opportunity."

Worthington's eyes widened.

"Hey, I'm always lookin' for an investment," Worthington said. "Whataya got?"

***

When Clint returned to the bar with Worthington in tow, Smith was holding court.

"Watch him," Clint said.

Worthington waved the bartender over. They each had a beer and watched while Smith charmed the people at the bar. Some of them even put their hands in their pockets.

"Is this for real?" Worthington asked. "Or is he a con man?"

"He's legitimate, as far as I can see," Clint said. "I've seen him do this in a museum, and a university, so far."

"And are they all as enthralled as these people?" Worthington asked.

"Most of them, yeah."

"What would my return be?"

"I'll put you together with him," Clint said, "and you can find out."

***

When Smith was finished with his crowd at the bar, Clint took Worthington over and introduced him.

"I was listenin' to your pitch," Worthington said. "Very impressive."

"A con man has a pitch, Mr. Worthington," Smith said. "A medicine man, a drummer. I'm none of those things."

Clint had heard Smith himself call what he had a "pitch," but he supposed the man felt he was the only one who could call it that.

"No, that's right," Worthington said, "Clint told me, you're a professor."

"That's right."

"Well, Professor," the gambler said, "why don't we go to a table and you can tell me what I'd be gettin' for my money—that is, if I decided to back you. I'll even throw in a drink."

"Well, now," Smith said, "that sounds like a pitch I can't turn down."

"I'll be right here," Clint said, as the two men walked away.

He watched them secure a table, then turned to the bartender and said, "Another beer."

"Comin' right up, Mr. Adams."

Chapter Fifteen

Somebody tried to kill Professor Henry Smith that night.

But it wasn't as simple as that . . .

***

Clint waited at the bar until Smith finished his talk with Sam Worthington. The gambler waved at Clint and returned to the back-room poker game. Smith came over to Clint.

"Any luck with Sam?" Clint asked.

"Yes, I think he's going to invest," Smith said. "He's thinking about it."

"Good. Ready to go back to the hotel?"

"Oh, yeah," Smith said. I'm beat from too much drinking and too much talking."

"And walking," Clint said. "We can get a cab right out front."

"Suits me."

It took five minutes, but then they were in a cab, headed back to the Palladium.

They walked through the lobby, paused at the bar, but kept going. They had both had enough to drink for the night.

Clint walked Smith to his room, made sure he went inside and locked the door.

"Breakfast in the morning?" Smith asked.

"I'll be there," Clint said. "Maybe we'll even go down the street."

"Won't that disappoint Alexandra?" Smith asked.

"Hey, you can always wait for her to finish work," Clint said.

"I'll think about it."

Smith went in, and Clint walked down to his own room. He looked up and down the hall before locking the door. He wished his room was closer to Smith's, but when he checked in, he didn't know he would be taking on a bodyguard position. Maybe a talk with the cooperative manager was in order.

He removed his boots, grabbed the book he was presently reading—Rudyard Kipling's *Kidnapped*, which had been a gift to him—and started reading.

He had been reading for about an hour when he heard the scream.

He sprang from the bed, grabbed his gun and ran into the hall. There he stopped, waiting to hear something that would tell him which direction to go in. Suddenly, he heard a noise from down the hall, where Smith's room was. Thumping, banging, the sounds of a struggle.

He ran down the hall and started knocking on Smith's door.

"Professor! Henry!"

Still the sounds of struggling inside, so he stepped back and kicked out once. His foot hit the door just below the knob, and the door slammed open.

Then it got quiet.

"Henry?"

It was dark in the room. There was only a shaft of light from the hall to go by. At the moment, it didn't reveal anything, so he stepped forward.

The hotel rooms had gas lamps on the wall by the doors. Clint reached up with his left hand and turned the gas up. The lamp lit the room, and he saw Henry Smith lying in the center of the floor.

"Henry?"

He didn't approach him right away. He looked around first, made sure nobody else was in the room, then went over to Henry Smith and leaned over him.

"Henry?"

He touched him to see if he was alive. Smith's eyes opened, he took a ragged, raspy breath and sat up. Clint could see the mark on his neck, like somebody had hanged him, except right in the center was a larger bruise.

"Henry? Are you all right?"

Smith focused his eyes on Clint, then said, "I-I think so."

Suddenly, Clint heard footsteps in the hall. He turned to the door, saw the desk clerk appear there.

"What's wrong? What happened?" the man asked.

"That's what I'm trying to find out," Clint said.

Other guests began to appear in the doorway.

"Get all those people back to their rooms," Clint told the clerk.

"Yessir. Come on folks, back to your rooms."

While the clerk herded the crowd away from the scene, Clint got Smith up off the floor and onto the bed, in a seated position.

"Can you tell me what happened?" Clint asked.

"I—I woke up and somebody was in the room," Smith said. "Next thing I know something was choking me."

"Did you see who it was?"

"N-no," Smith said, rubbing his throat.

"And what was around your throat?"

"I don't know for sure," Smith said. "But I can guess who it was, and what they were using."

"What?"

"It all comes down to one word."

"And what's that?"

Smith looked at Clint and uttered the word.

"Thuggee."

Chapter Sixteen

"Thuggees," Smith explained, after Clint had closed the damaged door as best he could. "They're actually called thugs, and deceivers. They're a sect of assassins. The word 'thuggee' really refers to the things they do, not who they are."

"Assassins," Clint said. "And one of them was in here trying to kill you."

"Apparently," Smith said, touching his neck. "He had this garrote of rope or cloth that they use, and it had some sort of weight right here." He touched his sore Adam's apple.

"Why kill you?"

"To keep me from going to India."

"But why?" Clint said. "I don't understand what the big deal is."

"They obviously don't want me to find anything when I go there," Smith said.

"But . . . where did this thuggee go?" Clint asked. "The door was locked, I had to kick it in."

"He had to use the window, then."

Clint walked to the window and examined it.

"It doesn't look like it's been opened," he commented.

"Well," Smith said, "he had to come in that way. And he must've gone out that way, or you would've seen him."

"The window doesn't look disturbed," Clint said.

"It's no wonder," Smith said. "These guys, they can scale walls like they do mountains."

"And get in locked windows?"

"If they want to," Smith said.

"Come on, Henry."

"Well, it's all part of the curse."

"You must know who's against you making this trip," Clint reasoned.

"Quite a few people, actually," Smith said, "from both countries."

"Okay," Clint said, "pack up your stuff."

"Where are we going?" Smith asked.

"You're going to spend the rest of the night in my room," Clint said. "In the morning we'll get two other rooms, right across from each other."

"And where are you going to spend the night?"

"Right here," Clint said. "To see if they try again."

"You've got be careful with these people, Clint," Smith warned, as he packed his bags.

"I intend to be," Clint said, "but they're on my side of the water right now, Henry. I'll worry even more about them when we get to theirs."

***

Clint walked Smith down to his room, and got him situated.

"I don't see how this will help," Smith said. "The Thuggees are notorious for getting their man, no matter what."

"We'll see," Clint said. "By the way, was that you who screamed?"

"What? Somebody screamed?"

"I heard them," Clint said, "That's why I came running."

"Well, it wasn't me," Smith said.

"Did your attacker scream?"

"I think I was almost out by then, if he did, I didn't hear him."

"Well, if they want you so badly, maybe they'll try again. If they do, I'll grab them—or him. Could it have been a woman? Because that's what the scream sounded like."

"No," Smith said, "the Thuggee followers are definitely men."

"Whoever they are," Clint said, "I'll be ready for them, this time."

"Okay," Smith said, "but that's not really making me feel any better. This is serious. You have to be very careful."

"Get a good night's sleep," Clint said. "Everything will look better in the morning."

"I hope so," Smith said.

Clint retrieved his boots, gunbelt, and the Kipling book to take with him to Smith's room.

"If you want me for anything, come down the hall, or yell," Clint said.

"Or scream?"

"Even that."

"Well, it wasn't me before," Smith said. "I wouldn't do that—and if I did, I wouldn't sound like a girl."

"I never thought you would," Clint said. "Now get a good night's sleep."

"Easy for you to say," Smith responded.

Clint left the room and went down to Smith's. He examined the door, discovered that the lock hadn't been damaged and still worked. It didn't make him feel very confident, since it had opened the first time he kicked it. But the Thug who attacked Smith may not have used the door. Clint still didn't see how he could have gone out the window and closed it behind him. There was definitely no access from outside.

How could a thug follower somehow have climbed a sheer wall?

Chapter Seventeen

Clint slept soundly through the night, and nobody tried to kill him, thinking he was Henry Smith. Now he just hoped nobody had killed Henry Smith, maybe thinking he was Clint.

He rose and dressed, quickly walked down the hall to check in with Henry Smith. The Professor opened the door immediately when Clint knocked.

"Boy, I'm glad to see you!" he said.

"And I'm glad to see you," Clint said. "I hope you got some sleep."

"I didn't think I would," he said, "but I did. Anybody could've broken in and killed me in my sleep. I was never so happy to wake up in my life."

"Let's take care of that," Clint said.

"How?"

"Breakfast," Clint said, "and some new rooms. Come on."

They went down to the lobby and, before leaving the hotel, met with the manager, again.

"Yes, I heard what happened last night," Lincoln said. "Of course, I'll have you both moved to different rooms. Side-by-side, or across from one another?"

"Good question," Clint said. "Make it across."

"Of course," Lincoln said. "It'll be done."

"And now," Clint said to Smith, "let's get that breakfast."

***

They went to a café down the street so they would only have to deal with food, and not Alexandra. Breakfast was a busy time in most eateries, and this was no different. They managed to wrangle a small table in the back that other people didn't seem to want.

After they ate, they had more coffee. Smith sat back and took a deep breath.

"Okay," he said, "I feel better."

"Still intend to keep all your appointments?"

"I have to," Smith said. "It's the only way I'm going to get to India."

"Okay," Clint said. "I don't have my list. What's on the agenda for today?"

"Noon I'm supposed to be talking to people in a park," Smith said. "Then, at three, another college."

"We might as well hire a cab for the day," Clint said. "Keep the same driver."

"Suits me," Smith said. "We can get it back at our hotel."

They paid their bill and walked back to the Palladium.

***

The driver they got was a young man in his twenties named Rufus Long.

"Well, sure," Rufus said, looking at the money in his hand, "I'm yours for the day. Hop in."

Clint and Smith climbed into the back of the open-air cab. Rufus climbed up into his driver's seat and picked up his horse's reins.

"Where to?"

"It's too early for your talk at the park," Clint said.

"That's okay," Smith said. "I've got another stop I want to make."

He gave Rufus an address, and they headed off.

***

"What's this place?" Clint asked. "It looks like another museum."

"Almost," Smith said. "The man who lives here was a friend of my father's. He has a huge collection of . . . stuff."

"What kind of stuff?" Clint asked.

"Among other things," Smith said, "some trinkets from India."

"Does he know you're coming?"

"No."

"Okay, then."

Rufus settled in to wait for them while they made their way up the driveway to the front door of the two-story mansion.

Smith knocked twice before the door opened and an older black man stared at them.

"Yes?"

"Lemual, do you remember me?"

The man stared at him with what seemed to be glazed over eyes.

"No," he said.

"Henry Smith," the Professor said. "Kenneth Smith's son?"

"Ken Smith?"

"That's right."

"You were little Hank?"

"That's right," Smith said. "You called me Hank."

"Come in, come in, sir," Lemual said. He was one of those black men Clint had seen many times, who could be sixty or eighty.

Once they were inside, Lemual embraced Smith and smiled, transforming his face. Even his eyes seemed to clear.

"Lemual, this is my friend, Clint Adams."

"It's a pleasure," Lemual said, shaking Clint's hand.

"For me, too."

"Is Everett here, Lemual?" Smith asked.

"Mr. Anderson is still here," Lemual said, "but he is not well."

"What's wrong with him?"

"The same thing that is wrong with me," Lemual said. "He's old."

Chapter Eighteen

"Can we see him?" Smith asked.

"He is asleep, but when he wakes I will tell him you're waiting. In the meantime . . . what brings you here?"

"I wanted to show my friend some of Everett's collection," Smith said. "Do you think he'll mind?"

"He enjoys nothin' more than showin' people what he has collected over the years," Lemual said. "And you are not just people. Come."

They followed Lemual through the house, which seemed to be stuffed with collectibles, even in the hallways and alcoves.

"My God," Clint said.

"I know," Smith said. "It's all through the house, but what I want to show you is behind locked doors."

"And I have the key," Lemual said, as they reached a set of double doors.

He inserted the key and turned.

"You may go in," he said to Smith. "I will go and check on Mr. Anderson."

As Lemual walked away Clint asked, "How long have they been together?"

"I'm not sure," Smith said. "Fifty, sixty years."

"And he still calls him Mister?"

"Above all, they respect each other," Smith said. "Come on, let's go in."

Smith pushed the double doors open.

"My God," Clint said, for the second time.

The room was huge, with ancient artifacts, weapons and animals hanging from the long sections of walls, and high ceiling.

"When I was a kid, this room fascinated me."

"It never scared you?" Clint asked.

"No, never."

"Then I guess you were born to do what you do," Clint commented.

"Come on," Smith said, "what I want to see used to be over here."

All around them were glass enclosed items, some of the cases vertical, others horizontal. Smith led him to one of the horizontal ones.

"These are from India," he said, pointing to the artifacts that were under glass.

Clint saw items of cloth, metal, and some that looked like rocks.

"What are they?"

"Arrowheads, pieces from cursed articles of clothing, and powerful minerals."

"Do you think something in this case killed your father?" Clint asked.

"If it did, Everett wouldn't have it here," Smith said. "He and my father were like brothers."

"Then why are we here?"

"I needed to check and make sure everything was still here, so nobody could use any of these items against me," Smith explained.

"And?"

"And it looks like they're all here," he said. "That's an enchanted arrowhead, that is a piece from a Maharaja's cloak, and those are cursed minerals from a fort in India."

"So you do believe in curses," Clint said.

"I do," Smith said, looking at Clint.

"Then why'd you make me think you had doubts?"

"I didn't want you to think I was crazy," Smith said.

"I don't," Clint said. "You can believe in whatever you like."

"And you?"

"Many Indian tribes believe in curses," Clint said. "I believe that if you think a curse can hurt you, it will."

"Hank?"

They turned, saw Lemual in the doorway.

"Mr. Anderson says he can see you, now. Please, follow me."

Lemual took them to the staircase in the main part of the house and up to the second floor. He led them down a hall to the master bedroom, where Everett Anderson was sitting up in bed.

"Henry?" he said. "Is that you?"

Unlike the black man, Anderson didn't carry his years as well. He must have been eighty, and looked it. His skin appeared as if it was parchment, but the smile on his face was real as he reached out to Smith.

"Uncle Everett," Smith said, approaching the bed.

They clasped hands, and Clint could see the genuine affection each had for the other.

"I'm so happy to see you, my boy."

"And I you, Uncle."

"And this is your friend?"

"Yes," Smith said, "Clint Adams."

"The Gunsmith," Anderson said, almost with reverence. "It's an honor." He looked at Smith. "Thank you for bringing him here, Henry. Now I can make him part of my collection."

"Uncle!"

Chapter Nineteen

Suddenly, both Everett Anderson and his man, Lemual, started laughing.

"I'm kidding," Anderson said to Smith and Clint.

"Uncle . . ." Smith said.

"Shall I have Lemual bring refreshments?" the old man in the bed asked.

"Not for me," Clint said. He didn't want to make the older black man carry a tray up the stairs.

"Me, neither."

"That'll be all, then," Anderson said.

"Yes, sir."

"Lemual still looks pretty spry," Smith said.

"Moreso than I do, I'm afraid," Anderson said. "These stick legs don't want to hold me, anymore."

"I took Clint in to see your collection."

"I hope you enjoyed it," Anderson said. "I, myself, don't get downstairs much, anymore."

"The collection seems to be the whole house," Clint commented.

"Indeed," Anderson said. "If I was ten years younger I'd have to buy a larger house, as I would still be collecting. But as it stands now, the contents have been pretty stagnant the past few years."

"I was especially interested in the items from India," Clint said.

Anderson looked at Smith with concern.

"Are you still looking for the curse that killed your father?"

"I'll be going to India, as soon as I get the backing," Smith admitted.

Anderson looked displeased, then started coughing. They waited for him to stop, and speak.

"I won't finance any of that trip for you," he said.

"I know that, Uncle," Smith said. "I just came to make sure none of your items were missing."

"My security is too good."

"Security?" Clint asked. "I didn't see anyone."

"Hassan handles my security," Anderson said. "You can meet him if you like, before you leave. Just tell Lemual."

"I'll do that," Smith said. "I'll let you know when I have a departure date, Uncle."

"Are you going alone?"

"I'll be taking the Gunsmith with me."

Anderson looked at Clint.

"That, at least, makes me happy," the old man said. "You will watch Henry's back?"

"Every step of the way, sir," Clint said.

"That's good," Anderson said, and then added, "though I don't know what good a gun will do against a curse."

"I guess we'll find out," Clint said.

***

They went back downstairs, where Lemual was waiting.

"Is there anything else I can do for you, sir?" he asked.

"Yes," Smith said, "we'd like to meet Hassan."

"Of course, sir," Lemual said. "You can wait in the library."

"Thanks, Lem. I know the way."

Smith led Clint to the library, which had all four walls completely lined with books.

"Do you know this Hassan?" Clint asked.

"No, he's new," Smith said. "That's why I want to meet him."

"When was the last time you were here?"

"Many years, as you could see when Lemual first looked at me."

Clint was about to comment when a black bearded man wearing a turban appeared in the doorway.

"I am Hassan," he said. "Lemual said you wanted to see me." He had a very deep voice.

"Yes," Smith said, "I'm Henry Smith, this is Clint Adams. We wanted to ask you about your security measures. Has anyone tried to break into the house, of late?"

"No," Hassan said. "I have been in charge of security for two years, and in that time no one has tried to break in."

"That's good," Smith said.

"Do you expect someone to try?" Hassan asked. "Shall I be extra vigilant?"

"I'm planning a trip to India," Smith said, "and I didn't want to think I might have to deal with any of these items, uh . . ."

". . . curses?" Hassan asked.

"Yes."

"If you are going to India, sahib, I would be wary of all curses."

"I intend to," Smith said.

"I understand from Lemual that your father was killed in India by a curse," Hassan said. "Do you know which one?"

"No, that's one of the things I hope to find out."

"I wish you much luck, sahib," Hassan said. He folded his hands, effected a bow, and backed out of the room.

Chapter Twenty

Lemual showed Clint and Smith to the door.

"Please stop by again," he said. "I haven't seen Mr. Anderson this perky in many months."

"I'll try to do that, Lem," Smith said. "Thanks."

They left the house, walked down the driveway to where Rufus was waiting with the cab. They got in the back and Smith gave Rufus the location of his first stop: Golden Gate Park.

"Okay," Clint said, as they sat back, "why don't you tell me what that was all about?"

"What do you mean?"

"We didn't go there to visit your long lost uncle, or to see a few trinkets," Clint said. "You've got to start being truthful, if you want me to help you. I mean, I'm not about to accompany a liar all the way to India."

"I guess I can't blame you for feeling that way," Smith said. "It was Hassan."

"What about him?"

"I told you I hadn't been to that house in a long time, but I keep tabs on it."

"How?"

"By telegram," he said. "I have some friends who drop me a telegram from time to time. The last time they did, it was when Uncle Everett hired Hassan."

"Okay, so it was Hassan," Clint said. "Did you get what you wanted?"

"No."

"What did you want?"

"After being attacked in my room by a thug, I just wondered . . ."

". . . if it was him?"

Smith nodded.

"How would he have known you were here?"

"It was in the newspapers."

"But how would he have known you were in my hotel?" Clint added.

"I don't know," Smith said. "Maybe he was watching."

"And why would he?"

"Look," Smith said, "I don't know anything about him. Why does he work for my Uncle Everett? Is he a member of a thug gang who doesn't want me to go to India?"

"You expected to know that when you saw him?"

"Well . . . I saw the hands of the one who tried to strangle me last night," Smith said. "I thought, maybe. . ."

"Did you see Hassan's hands?"

"No," Smith said, excitedly "did you notice how he kept them hidden. Either behind him, or in his pockets."

"I can't say I did," Clint said, "but I wasn't trying to get a look at his hands. I did notice he had a curved dagger in his belt. If he had wanted to kill you, why not use that, last night?"

"That's not the thuggee way," Smith said. "They have used blades and poison in the past, but they prefer strangulation—and from behind."

"Well," Clint said, "that didn't work, did it?"

"No, thanks to you interrupting him," Smith said.

"Do you still say that wasn't you who screamed?" Clint asked.

"No, it wasn't," Smith said. "I think it was him."

"Hassan?"

"Whoever tried to strangle me," Smith said.

"Well," Clint said, "maybe we should find out more about Hassan. Wouldn't Lemual tell you?"

"Lem is loyal to Uncle Everett. He doesn't talk about his business."

"So maybe we'll just have to talk directly to Hassan."

"Didn't we just do that?"

"I didn't know what you wanted, then," Clint said. "Now I do."

***

Golden Gate Park was filled with pine, cypress and eucalyptus trees. And a crowd was waiting for Professor Henry Smith to arrive.

There was a stage set up, with a podium, and whoever was hosting wasted no time introducing the Professor. Smith put on his bush hat and stepped to the podium.

Smith started his spiel, leading up to his pitch. Since Clint had heard it all before, he let his mind drift back to the meeting with Everett Anderson's security man, Hassan. Smith was right, the man had kept his hands out of sight the whole time. But Clint was sure that a man who wore that curved blade on his belt knew how to use it. If the need had arisen, those hands would have come into play fast enough.

Clint looked around, remembering what Smith had said about Hassan maybe watching them. Even if it wasn't Hassan, it could have been somebody he sent.

But everyone he could see was looking at the same thing—Professor Henry Smith. No one seemed to be paying Clint any attention. There wasn't even one pretty girl looking his way. They were all entranced by the handsome professor.

Clint thought about walking around for a better look, but in the end decided to stay put, close to Smith, since there had already been one attempt on his life.

Chapter Twenty-One

When Smith finished, he had to spend an hour with a line of people waiting to meet him, shake his hand, give him money or—in the case of some of the women—make a date.

Since all of the chairs were now vacated, Clint chose one and sat, continuing to watch Smith perform. That's what it had become in his mind, a performance. Anything the man had to say or do to raise the money to go to India and find his father's killer.

Why, Clint wondered, after all these years? Why go to India now?

When the last person in line had left, Smith walked over and sat down next to Clint. In the back row sat Rufus, who had decided to listen rather than wait in the cab.

"How did I do?" Smith asked.

"You had them all in the palm of your hand," Clint said. "Especially the women."

"I'm only interested in the ones with money," Smith said.

"How'd you do in that respect?"

"Okay, I hope," Smith said. "It's easy for people to make promises. Then you have to hope they keep them."

"Can we talk about something before we go?" Clint asked

"Sure," Smith said, "what's on your mind?"

"This trip to India," Clint said. "What's it for?"

"A dig," Smith said.

"Where, exactly?"

"Jaisalmer," Smith said. "It's also called 'The Gold City.' It's near the border of Pakistan."

"And what's there?"

"That's what I'm going to go and find out," Smith said. "Why all the questions, now?"

"Does this Gold City have anything to do with your father's death?"

"Gold City," Smith corrected. "Yes, there is a Curse of the Gold City. I'm concerned that it's what might have killed my father, but I'm not going to know for sure until I go there."

"Ah," Clint said, "so you're going to India to try to find out about your father's death."

"That's right."

"Well, why now?" Clint asked. "I mean . . . when did he die?"

"Ten years ago."

"Why didn't you go then?"

"Two reasons."

"I'm listening."

"One, Jaisalmer Fort hadn't been unearthed, yet."

"So somebody else dug it up?"

"Someone else found it," Smith said, "but I want to go and examine it."

"And the second reason?"

Smith hesitated.

"I've been afraid," he said, finally. "It's taken me ten years to build up the courage to go."

"That's pretty honest," Clint said. "Is that why you want me to go with you?"

"No," Smith said, "I'd already decided to go to India when I came to San Francisco to raise the money. Asking you for help was an afterthought—but one I'm glad I had."

"Well, we'll see if it turns out to be a good thing," Clint said. "I suppose we'd better get to your next appointment."

"Right."

They walked back to where Rufus was sitting.

"Hey, Professor," the young man said, jumping to his feet, "that was pretty good. Sounds like you have a pretty exciting life."

"It can be."

"Going to Egypt? And India? Sure sounds excitin' to me," Rufus said.

"Well, right now we're going to San Francisco University, which really isn't far from here." He looked at Clint. "I booked both these events because they were located so close together."

"Closer if you walked," Rufus said. "Right through there."

"You might as well take us," Smith said. "We've got some time to kill, and we'll want you to be there when I finish."

Rufus snapped the reins at his horse. They had him drive through the park, first, to get to the exit. By that time, they were further from the University, so it took some time to actually get there.

"Is this somethin' else I'd like to listen to?" Rufus asked, turning to face them after he had pulled to a stop in front of the building.

"It's more of the same," Smith said, "but you can listen, if you want."

"Naw," Rufus said, "I guess I'll just sit here and wait, this time. You almost had me goin' into my poke for ya, Professor."

They climbed down from the back of the cab and started for the building.

"You want to skip this one, too?" Smith asked.

"Actually," Clint said, "I skipped the last one. Didn't listen to a word then, and I won't now. I'll just watch."

Chapter Twenty-Two

More of the same . . .

There was a good crowd, much of it young and female. Clint doubted Smith would get much from them aside from admiration.

Once again he eyed the crowd, on the lookout for trouble, or the interest of others.

There were some university officials on the stage of the auditorium with Smith, and from the looks of them, they were as taken by the Professor as the students were. A university grant would go a long way toward getting Smith to India.

As with the park, Clint had to wait almost an hour for Smith to meet his "fans." By the time the professor walked over to where Clint was and sat down, he looked beat.

"You wouldn't think talking would be so hard," he said.

"Not for you, anyway."

"Yes, yes, I know," Smith said, "I talk a lot."

"I just meant," Clint said, "you're a teacher."

"Thanks. I think by the time we get back to the hotel, I'll be ready to eat."

"My thinking, too,"

They walked outside, hopped into Rufus' cab, and told him to take them to their hotel.

***

In front of the Palladium, Rufus reined his horse in, turned and said, "Is that it, gents?"

Clint leaned forward and gave him the money he had promised.

"Thanks!"

They stepped down.

"Again tomorrow?" Rufus asked.

"Come on by in the morning," Clint said, "and we'll let you know."

"See you then," Rufus said.

Clint and Smith turned to look at the Palladium, then Smith asked, "You got someplace in mind?"

"I do," Clint said. "Follow me."

***

Clint led Smith to a restaurant he had found during his first day's walk. There was a suppertime crowd, and they had to wait a short time for the kind of table they wanted.

The waiter was a homely man with muttonchops, but an expansive personality.

"First time here, gents?" he asked.

"Yes," Clint said, "it is, for both of us."

"You're gonna love it. We got us the best chef in town. In fact, that's his name above the door."

The name of the place was CHEF LEO'S, so that hadn't been hard to figure.

"What'll ya have?" the waiter asked.

"I'll have a steak dinner," Clint said, "and dress it up real good."

"We always do. And for you, sir?"

Smith looked around again, decided that what he wanted was not so outlandish for this place. He put his menu down.

"I'm in the mood for a rack of lamb," he said.

"Good choice, sir!" the waiter said. "It ain't on the menu, but the chef loves requests."

"Then can we request some coffee while we wait?" Clint asked.

"And beer with the suppers?"

"Both are no trouble," the man assured them. "I'll be right back."

***

"I still have this feeling I'm being watched," Smith said, during supper.

"Jesus, Henry, you were watched all day."

"No, I mean other than that," the professor said. "Somebody's watching me."

"Somebody who wears a turban?"

"I'm not kidding," Smith said. "I think the thugs are here to take care of me."

"Look, thugs, thuggees, whatever you want to call them, they're going to have to get past me to get to you."

"What if they don't see it that way?" Smith asked.

"And how would they see it?"

"Maybe they realize they're going to have to challenge you first. Maybe that's their intent."

"Nobody's tried that, yet," Clint said, "so relax. Enjoy that lamb?"

"How can I? Maybe they poisoned it."

Clint looked at Smith's plate, half of which had been devoured, already.

"Well," he pointed out, "if they had poisoned your food, you'd be dead by now." He looked down at his decimated steak. "And so would I."

"You're probably right," Smith said, picking up his knife and fork.

Chapter Twenty-Three

When they got back to the hotel, they were shown to their two new rooms. They were at the end of the second floor hall, across from each other, much larger than the other rooms they'd had. Clint checked the windows of both rooms, was satisfied that there was no access from outside—but that hadn't seemed to stop the thug who tried to kill Smith.

"What do you think?" Smith asked.

"Looks good," Clint said. "You want to get some rest?"

"I think so," Smith said. "Where will you be?"

"Right across the hall," Clint said. "How about a late supper? That'll give you a while to rest."

"Suits me," Smith said. "Sure I'm not keeping you from gambling?"

"I was using that as a distraction," Clint said. "But now I've got something else to do."

"Keep me alive?"

"You know it."

"Sounds good."

"Make sure you lock the door after I leave."

Clint stepped into the hall, waited for the lock to click, then went to his own room and did the same.

***

Clint tried to read, but ended up going over the day's events. He wished he had known about Hassan before they went to Everett Anderson's home. He would have paid more attention to the man's body language, his eyes and, of course, his hands.

It was clear that everyone was in that house—Anderson, Hassan, Lemual and Smith—believed in curses—especially this Curse of the Gold City. Clint was very much interested in going to India with Smith, and seeing the Gold City, and whatever else he could see.

He looked over at the book on the table next to the bed. The irony did not escape him that he was currently reading Rudyard Kipling. He may have been British, but Kipling had been born in India, and that had a heavy influence on his work.

And India was now having an influence on Clint Adams' life.

***

Clint woke with the Kipling on his chest. One look at the window told him it was dusk. He sat up, donned his boots and walked to the window. It was closed tight.

He left his room, crossed to Smith's door and knocked.

"I wake you?" Clint asked, when the professor opened the door.

"No, I've been up a while, but I feel rested."

"And hungry?"

"You know it."

"Then let's go."

"Wait."

Smith went back inside, then when he reappeared had a gun on his hip.

"Why the gun?" Clint asked.

"I've been thinking about Hassan, or whoever it was who attacked me. I don't want to be caught like that again."

"That's a big gun for somebody who doesn't usually wear one."

"It's European," Smith said. "It's called an automatic, the bullets go into a clip that slides into the handle."

"What the hell," Clint said, taking the gun from Smith and hefting it.

"It's a Schönberger-Laumann, invented by a man named Joseph Laumann." Smith took it back from Clint, and slid it into the holster. "And it won't be on the market for—oh, five or six years."

"Why do you have one?" Clint asked.

"It was a gift."

"That's a hell of a gift."

"Joseph's a friend," Smith said.

When they got to the lobby Clint said, "Let's stay inside."

"Fine. We'll say hello to Alexandra."

They entered the dining room, spotted the pretty waitress, who waved them to a table.

"Where've you fellas been hidin'?" she asked.

"I've been working, my sweet," Smith said. "Clint's been helping me."

"So, you two are workin' together, huh?" she asked. "The women in town better watch out for their hearts. Steaks?"

"Sounds good," Clint said. "And coffee."

"Me, too," Smith said.

"Comin' up, gents."

As she walked away Clint asked, "Two more talks tomorrow?"

"Yes," Smith said.

"And then what?"

"And then I take stock, see how much money I've got," Smith said. "With any luck, we can be on our way to India by the end of the week."

"And what if I pay my own way?"

"What? Why would you do that?"

Clint shrugged.

"Consider it my way of investing. Would that make it easier on you?"

"Well, yeah," Smith said. "I probably have enough now for myself, and my expenses. And once we get to India, the money we have will go further."

"You'll have to outfit yourself, won't you? For travel there?"

"Oh yeah," Smith said. "Pack animals, wagons, the whole works."

"And how much of the travel will be over desert?"

"Miles," Smith said. "In fact, it might even make more sense to go to Pakistan, first."

"Fine with me," Clint said. "I've never been to either place."

"It'll be a helluva experience for you," Smith said. "Especially if they're trying to kill us over there, too."

Chapter Twenty-Four

Alexandra fawned over Smith while serving them both their food. He found it embarrassing. Clint found it amusing.

Over coffee and pie, she and Smith flirted and when she walked away, Clint said, "Looks like you two are ready."

"Ready?"

"You'll have to tell her where your room is," Clint went on, "and be careful when you let her in, that nobody else is around."

"You really think she's going to come looking for me tonight?"

"I think she's ready," Clint said.

"Maybe it's you."

"I doubt it."

"Well," Smith said, watching Alexandra cross the room, "I can think of worse ways to occupy my time."

"We better get back," Clint said. "You want to be there when she comes, right?"

"Wait," Smith said, as Clint stood, "I've got to tell her what room I'm in."

"Good, you can do that while you pay the bill."

***

Hassan looked at the four men who stood before him. They were of a kind, tall, well-built, with black beards and turbans. They were all part of the Thuggee cult and, while in America, they served Hassan.

"Professor Smith has help," Hassan told them. "A man called the Gunsmith."

"He is a legend in America," one of the men said.

"No American legend can stand against the power of Kali," Hassan told hum. Kali was the Hindu Goddess of death and destruction. "And Kali is who we serve."

The four men fell to their knees in front of Hassan, the servant of Kali.

"What would you have us do?" one of them asked.

"Before we can take care of Smith, we must do away with Clint Adams," Hassan said.

"He can be shot from behind," another said.

"And which of you is as proficient with a gun as you are a blade?"

None answered.

"He must be taken care of the proper way," Hassan said. "You will use only your blade."

The curved blade Clint had seen on Hassan's belt had been a knife. The blades the four men wore were scimitars, curved swords.

"You must beware his weapon," Hassan said, "but you are Thuggee. You should have no trouble with him."

"And after it is done?" one asked.

"Come and tell me," Hassan said. "Come to the back door. I do not want Lemual to see you."

"And when will you dispatch Anderson and take back what is rightfully ours?"

"Soon," Hassan said. "First these two men must be dealt with. So go!"

They all stood and bowed before him, then turned and took their leave.

Hassan came out of the small house that stood behind the main home of Everett Anderson. At one time it was used by the caretaker of the estate, but there no longer was one. Now Hassan used it for his meetings with his men.

He had been working for Anderson for two years, just waiting, biding his time, and now it seemed as though the time had arrived.

He went back to the main house and entered through a rear door.

"There you are," Lemual said, coming into the kitchen. "Whatchoo been doin'? I been lookin' for ya."

"I am sorry, sahib," Hassan said, even as the words pained him. "What would you have me do?"

Chapter Twenty-Five

Smith wanted to get some air, so he and Clint walked past several well-lit and active casinos.

"Why don't we go in?" Smith asked.

"Do you gamble?"

"Not with money," Smith said. "I suppose I gamble with my life."

"I suppose that's true," Clint said, "with all the exotic places you go."

"But it's true of you, too," Smith said. "All you have to do is step outside and you're gambling with your life. Thanks to your reputation."

"There's not much I can do about that," Clint said. "But it might be different in India. Maybe I'll be able to walk about freely there, without being challenged.

"Ignored because, if you don't say you're the Gunsmith," Smith commented, "and don't talk about it, you might have some freedom."

"That would be nice."

"On the other hand, in cities in India, you don't have to be the Gunsmith to be challenged. They'll challenge anyone."

"Now you're giving me something to look forward to," Clint said, sarcastically. "Will we have any men with us?"

"I have one waiting there for us," Smith said. "His name is Sallah. He's travelled with me before."

"Okay, then at least we'll have one person there we can trust."

They went back to the hotel and stopped in the lobby.

"I should be okay in my room," Smith said. "Why don't you go out and spend some time in the casinos? There won't be any in India, you know."

"I'm used to there being no casinos around," Clint said. "I spend a lot of time on the trail. But I have a question."

"What's that?"

"About India," Clint asked. "Will we be riding camels?"

"Have you ever ridden a camel?"

"Once or twice, but not for very long. It's just that, since I've never been there, I'm wondering if I should bring my horse."

"Why not?" Smith replied. "He'll be as comfortable on a freighter as we will."

"A freighter?"

"That's how we'll go from here to India," Smith said. "That's what's in my budget."

"Well," Clint said, "I think I'll just go back to my room now and read."

"What are you reading?" Smith asked, as they went up the stairs.

"Kipling."

Smith laughed.

"Is that because you met me?"

"No," Clint sad, "I was reading him, anyway."

"How ironic."

They walked past Clint's room to Smith's where Clint waited while the professor went inside and locked the door. Then he walked back to his own door.

He stopped just outside.

Someone was in the room. He could feel it. He didn't think it was Tania, again, and the clerk wasn't letting anyone in.

He reached for the doorknob, but then backed off. Maybe he should just go to Smith's room. But as he thought that, a man appeared at each end of the hallway. They were wearing western garb, but had heavy black beards, and turbans rather than cowboy hats. They also had large, curved swords in their hands.

He had some choices. He could simply shoot them, and explain it to the law later. Or he could make a move they might not expect.

He reached for the doorknob and entered the room very quickly.

***

As Smith entered his room he locked the door, then turned and stopped short.

"Where've you been?" Alexandra asked. "I thought you'd come right back here after you ate." She was seated on the edge of the bed, one leg beneath her, the other leg rocking.

"Clint and I got some air," he said. "What're you doin' here, Alexandra?"

"I think you know," she said. "You and me, we been dancin' a dance, ain't we?"

"We've been flirting," he said, "but you should know I'll be going to India, soon. I can't be starting any kind of relationship."

"Oh pshaw," she said, "do you think I'm interested in a relationship? I just want to spend some time with the most excitin' man I've ever met."

"Oh," he said, taking a few steps forward, "well, I think we can do that."

Chapter Twenty-Six

As he had felt, there was someone in his room. Two more bearded, turbaned men were waiting, also holding long, curved swords.

"Hey, fellas," Clint said. "You got some friends out in the hall?" He locked the door.

The two men didn't speak. He heard footsteps out in the hall, that stopped in front of his door.

"I don't get this," he said to the two. "Didn't they tell you I have a gun? I could just shoot you."

Someone started to bang on the door.

"You are a coward?" one of them asked. "You would shoot us rather than fight?"

"Well," Clint said, "you do have swords."

The two men looked at one another. Behind him, the door was absorbing some punishment, but was standing up to it. The hotel had spent good money.

"We will wait," the spokesman said. "You get a sword."

"And then we'll fight?" Clint asked. "Four against one? Does that seem fair to you?"

"What do you propose?" the man asked.

"I think I should just shoot all four of you now," Clint said.

They didn't look concerned.

"You're thuggees, right?"

No answer.

"Maybe I should just talk to your boss," Clint said, then added, "Hassan."

"Move away from the door," the man said. "We will leave."

"You didn't come in through the window?"

They didn't respond.

"Okay." Clint stood aside, ready to draw his gun if they lunged at him. But they simply walked to the door and opened it. The spokesman held his hand up to the two in the hall to keep them from entering.

Then he looked at Clint.

"You get a blade," he said. "We will see you again."

"Are those thuggee blades?" Clint asked. "All curved like that? What are they called?"

"Scimitar," the man said, and stepped into the hall.

Clint stuck his head out and watched all four men walk off down the hall. When they disappeared, he walked back down to Smith's room. He heard sounds from inside, but they weren't fighting sounds. They were sounds he was used to. He could even hear the bed as it jumped up and down, noisily.

He went back to his room.

***

Inside Smith's room Alexandra was sitting on him, his hard cock buried deep inside her. She was bouncing up and down, her full breasts bouncing in front of him. She grunted every time she came down on him.

He reached for her breasts, her hips, ran his hands over her thighs. She was a woman in her thirties, not a girl, and she obviously had experience. Smith had been with women from all over the world, and this experience was right up there with the best of them. This woman knew there would be nothing between them after the sex.

Abruptly, he grabbed her, flipped her over, managed to do it without leaving her pussy. Once on her back, she smiled and spread her legs. He started ramming himself in and out of her. The bed began to hop up and down . . .

***

Clint went back to his room and once again locked the door. The four men with the swords had been sending a message. Maybe he should have sent one of his own, by shooting them. Of course, that would have brought the law running. And who knew how long that would keep him in San Francisco? Maybe long enough to miss a trip to India.

He assumed he had gained some time by mentioning Hassan's name. They were going back to their boss to get instructions on how to proceed. Clint had no intentions of obtaining a sword. If and when they did return, he wouldn't have much choice. He would have to shoot them, and deal with the ramifications later.

He was certain that the person Smith was bouncing up and down on his bed with was the waitress, Alexandra. And since she was a working girl, she wouldn't be spending the night. When they were done, she would leave both of them having gotten what they wanted from the other. She wasn't an impressionable young girl who was going to fall madly in love with the handsome adventurer.

And Smith certainly wasn't going to fall in love with her. Not when he had plans for India, and the curse that killed his father.

Clint decided to wait, and let Smith know about his visit at a later time. For now, he figured he'd let the man enjoy himself.

Chapter Twenty-Seven

When Clint heard the footsteps in the hall he went to the door and opened it. He was in time to see Alexandra going by, wearing the dress she had been wearing at work. However, it was now in a state of disarray, as was her hair. She smiled at him as she walked by.

"He's all yours now," she said. "But don't be so sure that won't be you, tomorrow. Good night."

He watched her hip-switch down the hall, obviously very happy with herself, then went to Smith's door and knocked.

"Clint," he said, looking embarrassed, "I was, uh—"

"I just saw Alexandra leave," Clint said, "so I know what you were doing."

Smith backed away from the door to let him in.

"But while you and Alexandra were moving the bed across the floor, I had some visitors."

"Oh? Who?" Smith laid back on his unmade bed. "Who?"

"I don't know their names, but they had beards, turbans . . . and scimitars."

"Scimitars?" He sat up, looking concerned.

"Yes," Clint said, "they're these curved swords—"

"I know what scimitars are," Smith assured him. "Are you all right?"

"Fine," Clint said. "They only wanted to talk, this time."

"Why didn't you shoot them?" Smith said. "I mean, I'm just asking."

"It would have been messy," Clint sad. "They were in my room."

"You mean while I—you were—they could've killed you while I—"

"They weren't going to kill me," Clint said. "There were four men with swords against one man with a gun. They knew how that would end."

"So what did they want?"

"I think they just wanted to take a look at me, see what they were dealing with."

"What happened?"

"We exchanged pleasantries," Clint said, "and then I told them to say hello to their boss, Hassan, for me."

"You said that?" Smith almost shouted, with a laugh. "What did they do? How did they react?"

"They didn't," Clint said. "They're very good."

"Well, they are thuggee. They'll be back."

"I know," Clint said, "and then I'll probably have to shoot them."

"Really?" Smith said. "I know where I can get you a scimitar. It'd be interesting."

"Just get some rest," Clint said. "And keep your gun close, in case they come for you next."

"But . . . you're right across the hall."

"That's right, across the hall," Clint said. "It would take me a few seconds to get over here."

"Right. Okay, I'll sleep with it under my pillow."

"Bad idea. It could go off in the middle of the night. Very messy. Just keep it close."

"Right."

"I'll see you in the morning," Clint said.

"What are you going to do tomorrow?" Smith asked.

"Well," Clint said, "other than your lectures, I thought maybe we'd have a chat with Hassan."

"What if it's not him?" Smith said, as Clint walked to the door.

"Wait." Clint stopped. "You said it was him."

"I said I thought it was him," Smith corrected. "I mean, I can't think of anybody else."

"Well, the best way to find out," Clint said, "is to ask him."

"You really think so?"

"We're going to find out," Clint said, "unless you come up with a better idea by tomorrow."

He went back to his own room.

***

Clint slept fitfully, waiting for thuggee to come through his window. In the morning he rose with first light, washed up in the room's small water closet and got dressed in clean trail clothes. He was about to leave the room when there was a knock at the door. With gun in hand, he answered it.

"Who is it?"

"It is Hassan," a voice said. "Can we talk?"

Clint was impressed. If Hassan was behind the attempt on Smith, and the boss of the four men from the night before, he was taking the bull by the horns before Clint and Smith could go to him.

Smart.

"Step back," Clint said. "Put your back against the wall."

"Very well."

Clint waited a few seconds, then opened the door, still with his gun in hand. Hassan was standing with his back pressed to the opposite wall. He was wearing a white suit of clothes, and his turban. He looked down at the gun in Clint's hand which, at the moment, was pointed at the floor.

"Still want to talk?"

"Yes."

"Then come in."

Chapter Twenty-Eight

Clint backed up so Hassan could enter, then closed and locked the door. The turbaned man looked around.

"Where is the Professor?" he asked.

"In a room down the hall."

"That is good," Hassan said. "I want to talk to you."

"So talk, but first, are we going to pretend that you didn't send those four men here last night? Or that you didn't try to have Smith killed in his room?"

"No pretending," Hassan said. "I am Thuggee. You have heard of us?"

"Yes."

"Good. Then you know this is serious."

"And do you know that this is serious?" Clint asked, lifting his gun.

"I know that you could kill me now with your gun," Hassan said. "That would not change things."

"So someone would still try to kill the professor?"

"Yes."

"To keep him from going to India?"

"To keep him from going to the Gold City, to be more precise."

Clint noticed the curved knife on the man's belt. He decided to tuck his gun into his belt.

"And what would be so bad if he went to the Gold City?" Clint asked.

"He would be putting his nose someplace it does not belong," Hassan said. "The curse of the Gold City would kill him."

"Then why not just sit back and wait for that to happen?" Clint asked.

"We do not need that kind of attention in Jaisalmer Fort."

"So what do you want from me?"

"Simple," Hassan said. "Let us kill him."

"Sorry?"

"Be finished with him," Hassan said. "And do not plan to go to India with him."

"Why would I do that?"

"If you do not," Hassan said, "you will also die."

"Is that a threat, or a promise?" Clint asked.

"It is a fact."

"I think you'll find that harder to accomplish than you imagine."

"We have many men, Sahib Adams."

"Then you're going to need them," Clint said.

"I came here as a courtesy."

"You came here to scare me," Clint said. "It didn't work."

"If you do not fear the thuggee, you are a fool," Hassan said.

"I'm just an American who's never been to India," Clint said. "Maybe once I go, I will be afraid."

"I assure you, by then it would be much too late," Hassan said, and left.

                              ***

The next knock that came was Professor Smith, just moments later.

"Was that Hassan I saw leaving?"

"It was."

"What'd he want?"

"Why don't we go to breakfast and I'll tell you," Clint suggested.

"I'm in favor of both of those," Smith said, "but let's skip the hotel dining room, huh?"

"Agreed."

                              ***

They walked about three blocks before stopping into an eatery they had not frequented before. Over eggs and coffee Clint told Smith about his talk with Hassan.

"Then he admitted it," Smith said. "He tried to have me killed."

"And he'll keep trying to kill both of us," Clint said.

"So what do we do?" Smith asked.

"We make it as hard as we can for him to accomplish," Clint explained. "And we show him that he would lose more than he gained if he keeps trying."

"How?"

"We'll figure it out," Clint said. "Right now, what time is your first appointment?"

"Nine a.m."

"Then we better get going," Clint said. "I'm sure young Rufus is waiting for us in front of our hotel."

***

When they got to the hotel, Rufus was indeed waiting in front.

"Ready, gents?" he asked.

"We're ready," Clint said.

"Then where're we headed?" the young man asked.

"Chinatown," Smith said.

Chapter Twenty-Nine

Clint thought Chinatown was an odd choice to try to raise funds.

"They're an exotic people," Smith explained, "who think about exotic locales."

"If you say so," Clint said, as Rufus drove down the Chinatown streets. This was as different from the rest of San Francisco as the Barbary Coast was. And both had their own level of crime, much of it right on the streets. Just during the ride, they saw three crimes being committed—one robbery, two assaults.

"You want to stop and help?" Smith asked when they saw the third one.

"No," Clint said. "Let's keep going."

The address turned out to be a two-story building apparently used for community meetings. As they stepped down from the cab, two Chinese men came out the front door.

"Mr. Smith," the older one said. "Welcome." They were wearing long, flowing robes. "Our people are very anxious to hear from you."

"Then let's get to it," Smith said. "This is my friend, Clint Adams."

"Clint Adams?" the younger one asked. "The Gun-smith?"

"That's right," Smith said.

"Why is he here?" the young one asked.

"He's a friend," Smith said. "He'll be making the trip to India with me."

"The Gunsmith?" the older one said. "In India? Very interesting. Will you talk about that?"

"No," Smith said, "that's just between us. We'd rather nobody knows who he is."

"Very well," the older man said, with a bow. "I am Master Chow, this is my nephew, China Chow."

"Nice to meet both of you," Smith said.

Neither of them offered a hand, just another bow, which Smith returned.

"Please, come inside," Master Chow said. Clint had the same problem with Chinese as he had with blacks. When they got to a certain age, they could be anywhere from sixty to eighty. Master Chow looked like he could be closer to the latter.

The Chows led them into the building, down a hall-way to yet another auditorium. There was no stage, but a podium at the front of the room. The seats seemed to all be taken by Chinese wearing either robes, or their paja-ma-like garments. Clint didn't know where these people were going to get the money to invest in Professor Henry Smith.

Seats had been left for them in the front row. Clint didn't like it, but there was no reason for anyone in Chinatown to want to kill him, but he would stay alert, anyway.

Master Chow stepped to the podium, explained that Professor Henry Smith was—"the infamous adventurer"—and then bowed to him. There was a smattering of applause.

Smith stepped up and made his pitch. When it was over, there was a smaller line than usual of people wanting to talk to him but when he came over to Clint at the end, he was smiling.

"This was a special batch of people."

"How so?"

"Master Chow's friends have money," Smith said, "and they're willing to invest."

"In return for . . ."

"That's what I have to find out," Smith said. "I think one of them wants me to take something with me."

"And deliver it at the other end?"

"Probably."

"Do you want to do that?"

"It depends on the money."

"When will you know?"

"When I hear from Master Chow."

"Okay, then. What's next?"

"You won't believe me."

"Try me."

"The Barbary Coast."

***

Clint wondered what the chances were they would get shanghaied while on the Barbary Coast for Smith to seek investors.

"What's this place going to be?" Clint asked.

"One of the bigger saloons," Smith said. "The Queen of Hearts."

"Could be worse," Clint said.

"How?"

"It could be the Bucket of Blood."

***

Rufus pulled to a stop in front of the Queen. The streets of the Barbary Coast were always busy, but the saloons usually came alive at night. The front doors of the Queen looked to be closed and locked.

"You sure this is the place?" Rufus asked.

"This is it," Smith said. "We just have to knock."

He and Clint got out of the cab.

"Wait?" Rufus asked.

"Yes," Smith said.

Rufus looked at Clint.

"You'll be all right," Clint said. "They're waiting for the Professor."

Rufus nodded, but he didn't look too happy.

Chapter Thirty

A man in a three-piece suit answered their knock on the front doors.

"Professor?" the man asked.

"Yes."

"I'm Kevin Hawkins."

They shook hands.

He looked like a businessman in his fifties, but when he turned toward Clint there was something different in his eyes. He hadn't always been a businessman.

"And him?"

"He's with me."

"I need a name."

Smith looked at Clint.

"My name is Clint Adams."

"The Gunsmith Clint Adams?" Hawkins asked. "That one?"

"It's the only one I know."

"What are you doin' here?" Hawkins asked.

"It's like the Professor says," Clint replied. "I'm with him."

Hawkins studied the two of them for a few moments, then said, "Come on in."

The Queen of Hearts was a large spacious saloon, with a theater right next to it. Hawkins led them to the theater, where people were already seated. Most of the men present were wearing suits like the one Hawkins wore. There were no women.

"Let me just introduce you," Hawkins said. "Mr. Adams, you can sit down front."

"I'll stand, thanks," Clint said, and did so, off to the side of the stage and podium, his hands clasped in front of him. It was a simple position to draw from, if it became necessary.

"Ladies and gentlemen," Hawkins said, standing at the podium. "If I can have your attention. Our guest of honor has arrived. He's a world renowned archeologist and adventurer, and is here to talk about his newest venture. So, with no further delay, let's welcome Professor Henry Smith."

Smith walked to the podium. Once there he had to wait for the applause to die down before he started speaking.

"Thank you, Mr. Hawkins for inviting me, and thank you all for attending . . ."

Clint watched the crowd while Smith spoke. Their faces were expressionless. He wondered how any of them actually owned businesses on the Barbary Coast, and how many were in attendance for the pitch?

He had listened to Smith at least four times now. The man compared well to carnival barkers and medicine men he had heard in the past. Clint could see the people in the audience responding. He thought it would be ironic if most of Smith's investors came from Chinatown and the Barbary Coast.

When Smith finished he stood there absorbing the applause, while Hawkins came and stood alongside him. After they shook hands, Smith went to the end of the stage to greet his fans and potential investors.

Kevin Hawkins came down and stood next to Clint.

"He's quite a man," he said.

"Yes, he is."

"How long have you been friends?"

"Not long at all," Clint said.

"But you're going to India with him?"

"Sounds like a whole new adventure for me."

"Oh, it will be," Hawkins said, "I guarantee you that."

They both continued to watch Smith interact with members of the audience.

"Have you been to India?" Clint asked.

"No," Hawkins said, "I just think it'll be something totally different for you."

Clint scanned the audience.

"Are you looking for someone?" Hawkins asked.

"Just trouble," Clint said. "It seems to follow me around."

"Do you think it will follow you to India?" Hawkins asked.

"I hope not."

When Smith had shaken hands with the last potential investor, he walked over to where Clint and Hawkins were standing.

"I hope that was what you wanted," Smith said to Hawkins.

"It was even more," the man said. "You made *me* want to go with you. I'll be donating to your war chest."

"Well," Smith said, "I hope some of these people feel the same way."

"They will, don't worry," Hawkins said. "Have you made any other pitches around town?"

"One or two," Smith admitted.

"No need to sound apologetic," Hawkins said, "I knew this wasn't the only one."

"Good."

"Where are you staying. I'd like to messenger over the money for you."

Smith looked at Clint, who nodded.

"The Palladium."

"Just outside of the Square. I know it," Hawkins said. "I'll send word."

Chapter Thirty-One

Hawkins offered Clint and Smith drinks on the house, so they accompanied him to the saloon while people were filing out of the building.

The saloon was still empty, except for a big, brutish looking bartender cleaning the bar top with a rag.

"Hey, Jumbo," Hawkins said.

"Boss," the bartender said, and drew three. "There ya go."

"Thanks, Jumbo."

Jumbo walked down to the other end of the bar. Hawkins turned to face Clint."

"Jumbo?" Clint asked.

"What else would you call him?"

"What's his real name?"

"Woodrow," Hawkins said. "Wouldn't you rather be called Jumbo?"

Clint laughed.

"I suppose."

Hawkins looked at Smith.

"So, when do you two leave for India?"

"As soon as I have enough money to book our passage on the freighter."

"You're taking a freighter?"

"It's the safest way."

"Which one?"

Clint raised his finger before Smith could reply.

"It's also safer if we keep that information to ourselves," he said.

"Of course, of course," Hawkins said.

"And we have to get going," Clint said. "Still many plans to be made for the trip."

"Well, thanks for coming by, Professor," Hawkins said. "I'm sure you'll be hearing from some of us."

"I hope so," Smith said.

He and Clint turned and went out the front doors to where Rufus was waiting. He apparently wasn't as afraid as he first had been, for he was dozing off.

"So what next?" Smith asked. "I have no more appointments today."

"Something occurred to me," Clint said.

"What's that?"

"We told him what hotel we're in."

"That's so anybody wanting to invest can find me," Smith said.

"I know," Clint said. "But that means you also told others, right?"

"Right."

"Then I think we need to change hotels, right now."

"If we do, how are they going to find me to give me money?" Smith asked.

"We'll make arrangements," Clint said.

They climbed into the cab, woke Rufus and told him to take them back to their hotel.

***

By the time they got to the Palladium, Clint was feeling foolish. He should have thought of moving to another hotel even before Hassan had sent the four visitors. Everybody who had heard Smith speak the last two days knew—then he realized that was wrong, because he had already moved Smith once. So it was only the people from Chinatown and the Barbary Coast who knew about the Palladium.

As they got out of the cab in front of the hotel Clint asked Smith, "What did you tell them when we took you out of the Bella Union?"

"To hold any messages for me and I'd pick them up," Smith said. "And that reminds me, we've got to do that."

"Okay," Clint said, "but first let's get you moved . . . again."

***

The manager wasn't happy, but understood.

"We don't want another attack in your hotel," Clint said. "Innocent people might get hurt."

The man agreed, and also agreed to hold any messages for them.

Clint and Smith carried their gear out to Rufus' cab.

"Where to?" the young driver asked.

Clint wanted to use a hotel he had never been in before.

"You tell us," he said.

"What?"

"We don't want a hotel here in the Square," Clint said. "or in Chinatown, or on the Barbary Coast. So you take us somewhere."

"Somewhere cheap?"

"Let's say reasonable," Clint replied, "and clean."

"I can do that," Rufus said.

"Then let's go!"

***

Rufus drove for about twenty minutes and stopped in front of a hotel on Powell Street, not far from Union Square.

"Nobody's gonna find you here," he told Clint and Smith.

"Did anybody follow us from the Palladium?" Clint asked.

"No, I made sure that didn't happen."

"Good," Clint said. "Can you wait?"

"I'm still all yours, Mr. Adams."

Clint and Smith went into the Truxton Hotel, which Clint had never heard of. They registered for two rooms under assumed names. Henry Smith used Brown, and Clint used Jones. They also managed to secure rooms across from each other, and away from the front of the hotel. Outside of both of their second-floor windows was a sheer drop to the street.

The rooms were small, and clean. It might not have been one of San Francisco's fanciest hotels, but it still had the new inside toilets. One thing Clint didn't miss about the "Old West" were the outside latrines and outhouses.

Clint stowed his gear in his room, walked across the hall and knocked on Smith's door.

"Are we set?" Clint asked.

"I'm fine," Smith said, "but I wish we had stopped at the Bella Union for messages. Depending on what they have for me, I might have hit my goal."

"No problem," Clint said. "We've got plenty of the day ahead of us, and we have Rufus."

Chapter Thirty-Two

Their first stop was the Bella Union for messages. Clint entered with Smith, who went to the desk to collect them. He didn't open and read any until they got back to their cab.

"Well?" Clint asked.

"Some big investors," Smith said, with satisfaction. "Looks like we're not very far from our goal." He folded up the messages and tucked them into a shirt pocket. "What we see from today's meeting might do the trick."

"So we'll check the Palladium tomorrow for messages," Clint said. "Do you have any more meetings scheduled?"

"No," Smith said, "I've made all the pitches I can. Now it's just a matter of putting everything together, and I think I can."

"Then all that's left is to make the trip arrangements," Clint said. "Get the supplies."

"And we just have to wait and see what Hassan and his thuggees throw at us to keep us from making that freighter," Smith added.

"Maybe we don't," Clint suggested.

"What do you mean?"

"Well," Clint said, "instead of waiting, we could take the fight to them."

"Do you know where the four men are?" Smith asked.

"No," Clint said, "but we know where Hassan is."

"You want to go back to Everett's house?"

"Maybe your uncle, or Lem, can tell us something we can use," Clint suggested. "It's worth a try."

"Okay with me," Smith said.

"Good," Clint said, "because I doubt I could get into that house without you." Clint sat forward, slapped Rufus on the shoulder, and they were off.

***

"What's going on?" Rufus asked.

They came around the corner, within sight of the Everett Anderson house, and saw the police.

"Stop here," Clint said. "We'll go over and find out."

He and Smith got out of the cab and walked toward the house. There were uniformed police all over the place, San Francisco's modern police department at work.

"Hold on there," one of them said, putting his hand up. "Nobody can go near the house."

"I'm family," Smith said, "Everett Anderson's my uncle. What's going on?"

The policeman looked at them, then said, "Wait here."

He went into the house, came out with two men who were not in uniforms, but were wearing suits.

"You gents say you're family?" one of them asked. He was the taller, older of the two.

"He is," Clint said, pointing. "I'm just a family friend."

What are your names?" the shorter, younger one asked.

"I'm Professor Henry Smith. This is Mr. Adams." Clint noticed that Smith had kept his first name out of it, for now. "Adams" was a common enough name. "Who are you gents?"

"I'm Detective Saunders," the tall man said," and this is Detective Louderbach, San Francisco police."

"Why are the police here?" Smith asked. "Burglary? Were some of Uncle Everett's collection taken?"

"His collection?" Saunders said. "What did he collect?"

"Everything," Smith said, "anything old."

"Weapons?"

"Some."

"Is he all right?" Clint asked. "There's a lot going on here."

Saunders eyed both of them, then looked at Smith.

"I'm sorry," he said, "but your uncle is dead."

"He was in bad health when I saw him last," Smith said. "How did he—"

"He was killed."

"How?" Clint asked.

"Strangled," Saunders said.

"From behind," Lauderbach added, speaking for the first time. "Any idea who would want to do that?"

"I don't know," Smith said. "Strangled?"

"From behind," Saunders said.

"What about Lem?" Smith asked. "Did you check with him?"

"Is that his black man servant?" Saunders asked.

"Yes."

"Yeah," Lauderbach said, "he's dead, too. Also strangled from behind."

"With what?" Clint asked.

"We don't know," Saunders said. "No real marks on the neck, except for a bruise, here." He touched his own adam's apple. "So it doesn't look like a rope was used."

"Jesus," Smith said. "So, was somebody robbing the house and then they decided to—"

"Maybe you can help us with that," Saunders said. "If we let you inside, could you tell if something was missing?"

"Maybe," Smith said. "What about Hassan?"

"Who?" Lauderbach asked.

"Hassan," Clint said. "He handled security."

"There was only the two men in the house," Saunders said. "Anderson and the old black man. We found him downstairs."

"Okay, then," Clint said. "Let us in and we'll see what we can tell you."

As the four of them started walking toward the house, Saunders said, "Tell us more about this Hassan."

Chapter Thirty-Three

In the house they saw Lem lying on the floor in the entry way. He was on his back, and his eyes were wide open.

"Damn it," Smith said.

"Did you know him well?" Saunders asked.

"Pretty well," Smith said, "Although I hadn't seen him for years."

"Why would somebody kill him?"

"Because he was in the way?" Smith asked.

"That's what we were thinking," Saunders said. We might as well go upstairs."

He led the way up the steps, with his partner taking up the rear. They went down the hall to Everett Anderson's bedroom, where Saunders stopped and turned.

"Look," he said, "don't touch."

"Right."

He stepped aside and allowed them to enter.

Clint and Smith walked to the bed and looked at the dead old man. His eyes were also open, as was his mouth. Clint could see the bruise on the adam's apple.

"Uncle Everett," Smith said, shaking his head.

"What about Hassan?" Saunders asked, coming up behind them. "Who is he, what is he, where is he?"

"He's from India," Smith said. "He was working for my uncle, doing security."

"Not very good at his job, was he?" Lauderbach asked.

"Doesn't look like it," Clint agreed.

"Where is he?"

"I don't know," Smith said. "I thought he lived here."

"There's a smaller house out back," Saunders said. "Could that have been his?"

"Maybe."

"We'll check it," Saunders said. "Let's go downstairs so you can have a look around, see if anything is missing."

Clint and Smith exchanged a glance. They wanted to talk to each other, but there wasn't going to be a chance until they left the house.

"Okay," Smith said. "Let's have a look."

***

Back downstairs Saunders and Lauderbach walked Clint and Smith around the house.

"This is a collection?" Lauderbach asked. "Looks like a bunch of junk."

"You have to forgive my partner," Saunders said. "He's got no class."

"This stuff is class?" Lauderbach echoed.

When they got to the locked doors of the main collection Saunders asked, "You got a key?"

"No."

"What's in there?"

"My Uncle's most expensive items."

"Oh well," Saunders said, "then we have to get in there and have a look."

"Lem should have a key on him," Clint pointed out. He also wanted to get a look inside.

"I'll go and check," Lauderbach said.

Clint, Smith and Saunders waited there for the other detective to return.

"When was the last time you were here?" Saunders asked.

"A couple of days ago," Smith said. "First time in many years."

"Did you come to San Francisco to see him?"

"No," Smith said. "I'm going to India, taking a freighter from here. I thought I'd stop in and see him while I was in town."

"How did he seem?"

"Sick, frail," Smith said. "Didn't look like he had much more time. I don't know why somebody would kill him."

Lauderbach came back with Lem's keys, tried a few before he found the right one. When he swung the doors open, they could see the room was a wreck, as if a stampede had gone through it.

"Maybe this is why somebody killed him," Saunders said.

Chapter Thirty-Four

Clint could see the look of horror on Smith's face as he took in the maelstrom of the room.

"What a mess," Saunders said. "Not always like this, I'll bet?"

"Not at all," Clint said. "I've only been here once, but everything was in order."

"Mr. Smith?" Lauderbach said.

"Professor?" Saunders called

"Give him a minute, will you, boys?" Clint asked. "This is a shock."

"Then maybe you can tell us about this Hassan, Mr. Adams," Saunders said.

"He's tall, has a black beard and wears a turban," Clint said.

"A turban?" Lauderbach said.

"It's a thing they wear on their head—" Saunders started then stopped. "Never mind. What else?"

"He was supposed to be working security for Mr. Anderson."

"How long?"

"Two years."

"You think he was behind this?"

"Yes."

"How can you tell?"

"He likes to strangle people."

"What?" Lauderbach asked.

"It's an Indian thing."

"Indians are involved?" Lauderbach asked.

"Indians from India," Clint said.

Lauderbach stared at him, then brightened.

"A turban!"

"Right."

Smith was walking around, looking at the devastation.

"Hassan has a group of men who like to strangle people," Clint said. "They tried it on the Professor, and then on me."

"On you?" Saunders asked. "You kill 'em?"

"No," Clint said, "I talked them out of it, but that won't work again."

Now Saunders and his partner looked over at Smith.

"So Professor? Anything missing?"

Smith came walking over.

"I can't tell," he said. "I was only in here once in the past . . . twenty years."

"And can you tell us where to find Hassan?"

"I would've said here," Smith said. "If he's not here . . ." He shrugged helplessly.

"You two haven't really been a big help," Detective Saunders said.

"I've told you all I know," Smith said.

They looked at Clint.

"And I suppose you're going to say you don't know anything," Saunders commented.

"He knows more than I do," Clint said.

"Then I think the two of you better leave," Saunders said. "We have work to do."

"But if we—" Smith started, only to be cut off by Clint grabbing his arm.

"You're right. We'll be going, Detective," he said. "Thanks."

Clint pulled Smith along with him through the house and out.

***

"Jesus," Smith said, when they were outside, "that crazy Hassan killed Uncle Everett and Lem."

"And you know what that means?" Clint asked.

Smith stared at him.

"We're next," Clint said.

"What do we do?"

"We've got to get to Hassan and his men before they get to us."

"There's another problem," Smith said.

"What's that?"

"The cursed objects I showed you when we first went into the room? They're gone."

"And you didn't tell the police?"

"I would've sounded crazy," Smith said. "You think two detectives in a new modern police department are going to believe something like that?"

"You might be right."

"Hassan's gone crazy," Smith said. "We can't let him get away with this."

"This might have been his long term plan," Clint said. "To eventually kill your uncle."

"What for?"

"Those cursed items," Clint said. "Or whatever items your uncle could get his hands on."

"Or me?"

Clint nodded.

"Maybe you," he said.

"So how do we find him?"

"We don't," Clint said, as they approached Rufus' cab, "we let him find us."

Chapter Thirty-Five

Back to the Bella Union, Smith's first hotel, where they both got rooms.

"Now we have to go the other way," Clint said, as they rode back with Rufus.

"What do you mean?" Smith asked.

"We switched hotels to hide you," Clint said. "Now we have to be out in plain sight."

"Is that wise?" Smith asked. "What if they try to kill us from a distance?"

"Will they use guns?" Clint asked. "I mean, is that a thuggee thing?"

"Knives, poison and strangulation. That's pretty much their holy trinity."

"Then they have to get close enough."

"Which they won't do because of your gun."

Clint looked down at his sidearm.

"You're right," he said. "I just may have to put this down, only without them knowing it's deliberate."

"If they're from India, they may not necessarily know your rep. I mean, to the extent it goes."

"You might be right. Although I got the idea from Hussan that he pretty much knew who I was. I just didn't think he cared."

"He did seem . . . unflappable."

While they were back at the Bella Union, they also let Rufus go. They didn't want the young man getting hurt. Hassan had already proven nobody was safe.

"So, are we going to sit in our hotel and wait?" Smith asked.

"No, we're going to go out and eat, and hit some of the saloons and casinos."

"That sounds good," Smith said. "After all the pitches I've made, and what happened to Uncle Everett, I could stand to let go a little."

"Well, let's make it just a little," Clint said. "We can't afford to be too drunk, or too involved with gambling. We want to be targets, but not sitting ducks."

"I understand."

"We might as well check in at the Alhambra first, and see how the back-room poker game is doing, now that I'm not there. Somebody else must be racking up the chips, by now."

"Good," Smith said, "I could use a drink—I know, I know, but just a bracer, after seeing Uncle Everett and Lem like that."

***

Clint was used to walking around with a target on his back, he just wasn't used to painting it on there, himself.

And all he had to back him up was a professor who admitted he wasn't very good with a gun.

On the other hand, the men who might be taking advantage of the target didn't use guns. So unless they were going to try to poison or strangle him, he could expect a knife in the back. And from a distance, that wasn't an easy thing to do—unless you were Jim Bowie. Clint had known Kit Carson, another man who could throw a knife with deadly accuracy, but there weren't too many others.

They entered the Alhambra, which was in full swing that early in the evening.

"Where's this poker game you've been talking about?" Smith asked.

"It's in a back room," Clint said. "We'll have a drink first, before we check on it."

"Will they let a stranger sit in?"

Clint looked at Smith.

"You play?"

"I've played poker in Tokyo, Japan, Sidney, Australia and Madrid, Spain. Yes, I've played a time or two."

"High stakes?"

"Well, no," Smith admitted, "I couldn't justify betting the money people had invested."

"Unless you were looking to double it."

"Or I could lose it all."

Clint grinned.

"That's why they call it gambling."

They walked to the bar, where the bartender recognized Clint.

"Haven't seen you lately," he commented.

"Been busy," Clint said. "How about two beers?"

"Comin' up."

Once they had their beers they turned and surveyed the place.

"It'll be hard for Hassan's thugs to sneak up on you in here," Smith said. "Not unless they take off their turbans."

"Do they ever do that?" Clint asked. "Work without their turbans?"

"They're very controlled by their faith, their religion," Smith said.

"So that's a no?"

"If we were in India, I'd say yes. Since we're here in the U.S., I don't know."

"Great," Clint said. "Does that mean they may even decide to shave, and use guns?"

"I hope not."

So did Clint. Without the beards and turbans, they could be anyone in the room.

"Okay," Clint said, "let's look in on the game."

They put their empty mugs on the bar and walked across the room.

Chapter Thirty-Six

Sam Worthington answered the door.

"Hey," he said, "people been askin' about you."

"What people?"

"Other players," Worthington said. "They're tired of losin' to this guy, Gallagher. They want you to come in and best 'im."

"What happened to Al Cody?"

"He's here, holdin' his own," Worthington said. "Who's your friend?"

"Professor Smith," Clint said. "He's okay."

"If you say so." Worthington let them in and locked the door.

Clint looked over at the table, saw Cody and Gallagher, two faces he knew, and two he didn't.

"New blood?"

"They came in last night," Worthington said. "They play no better than the two they replaced. They've got the money, but not the skill."

"Lot of those around," Clint said.

"Can you sit back in?" Worthington asked.

"Not today," Clint said. "I just came by—"

"Just for an hour or so," the man argued. "It might change the flow of the cards. If you do, I'll limit the games to stud."

"Go ahead, Clint," Smith said. "I can watch."

"Player coming in!" Worthington announced, rushing the table.

***

It was fairly easy for Clint to concentrate, since in that room they were safe from any thuggee attacks. Unless one of the two new players at the table was a thug. Clint studied them and decided they were not. For one thing, both of the men were overweight businessmen.

After a few hands Clint could see what Worthington meant. Al Cody and Jack Gallagher were the only players who showed any sort of skill. They not only played their cards, but the players, as well. It was the sort of thing Bat Masterson and Luke Short made sure Clint learned about poker. Years later both said they were sorry they had shared their knowledge with him. He had gotten too good—though not so good he could beat those men on a regular basis. Bat and Short were still the best poker players Clint had ever seen—and that included Hickok and Doc Holiday. Both of those men had been good, but too impatient. They had also both died too young.

After an hour, things had gone the way Worthington had hoped. Clint took some hands that either Cody or Gallagher might have taken had he not been there. The other players were still losing, and one of the overweight businessmen withdrew. Worthington then reinstituted draw poker as an option.

Rather than have a house dealer, the game was passing the deal from player-to-player. As soon as Gallagher got the deal, he called "Draw," and dealt five cards to each player.

Clint spread his cards and found himself looking at three sixes. He looked at the other players, immediately knew that two of them had nothing. Cody and Gallagher were harder to read, although Clint thought he had Gallagher figured out. He slow-played his good hands, preferring to wait 'til the end of the hand to sandbag his opponents.

Clint was pleased that Cody opened. He simply called, as all the other players did, including Gallagher.

"Cards," Gallagher said.

"One," Cody said, which pretty much solidified that he had two pair.

The three players between Clint and Cody all took three cards. Clint was fairly sure they were trying to build something. If one of them got lucky and did, he would bet it.

Clint said, "Two," not hiding anything.

Gallagher said, "I'll play these." He had a pat hand, but hadn't raised, preferring to keep everyone in the game. He could have a straight, flush or full house.

Clint looked at his cards with satisfaction. You knew your luck was good when you were facing a pat hand, and improved your own.

Cody was the opener, so the bet went to him.

"Fifty," he said, tossing his chips in.

The three players between Cody and Clint all said, "Fold." They had all tried to build on nothing and failed.

Clint said, "Call," and left the play up to Gallagher.

"Your fifty," the man said to Cody, "and two hundred more."

Clint knew that men like Cody and Gallagher—professional gamblers—played in games of this magnitude weekly. He, however, picked his spots to splurge with his money, this way. San Francisco was one of those spots.

He watched Cody as the man tried to decide what to do. That was odd, because Cody usually knew ahead of time what his move was going to be. This meant he had a good hand, but was it good enough to face a pat hand?

"I'm gonna call you," he said, finally.

"I'll call," Clint said, "and raise two hundred."

Gallagher stared at Clint. He had been worried about Cody. Now he had to wonder what Clint had.

"I'll call your two and raise five," Gallagher finally said.

"That's a big bet," Cody said. "I'll leave this up to you two."

The buy-in for this game had been ten thousand. Gallagher and Cody had walked in with that much in their pockets. Clint had gone to the bank to withdraw it from one of his accounts days before. Over the years he had gone into businesses—mines, stores, saloons—with friends all over the country. Some prospered, some didn't, and his cut was always deposited for him. He knew he wasn't being cheated, because he went into business with men he could trust.

Now Cody, Gallagher and Clint all had more than their buy-in on the table in front of them.

"Five hundred, huh?" Clint said.

"That's right."

"I didn't see Tania at the tables out there, Jack," Clint said.

"Never mind Tania," Gallagher said, "Make your play, Clint."

"I'm going to call your five hundred," Clint said, "and raise a thousand."

"You don't make bets like that," Gallagher said.

"I don't?"

"No," Gallagher said, "you're a talented amateur, not a pro."

"Hey," Clint said, "cards are cards."

"Your thousand," Gallagher said, "and two more."

"I'm going to call, Jack," Clint said, "and leave it at that, because I don't want to clean you out."

"I appreciate it," Gallagher said, sarcastically. He laid his hand out. "Heart flush to the king."

"Nice," Clint said, laying his hand out. "Three sixes and two eights. I think they call that a full boat."

"Fuck," Gallagher grunted.

"I knew he had you," Cody said, with a smile as Clint raked in the pot.

"Yeah? How'd you know that?"

"I've been sittin' here playin' with him for three days," Cody said.

"Why didn't you say something?"

"Would you have changed your play if I did?" Cody asked.

"With a pat flush?" Gallagher asked. "No."

The cards passed to Cody, who said, "Five card stud."

***

Clint played for another two hours, and then quit for supper. By that time, Gallagher's stack was way down. Most of the chips were in front of Clint and Cody.

"You better be comin' back," Gallagher said.

"I'll be back," Clint assured him. He just didn't know when.

At the door, Sam Worthington said, "Thanks. That changed the game."

"It was that pat hand of his that changed it," Clint said.

"*Will* you be back?" Worthington asked. "Or should I put your chips in the safe?"

"Just set them aside," Clint said. "I'll be back at least once more before I leave town."

"That's good enough for me," Worthington said.

As Clint and Smith left the room and re-entered the saloon, the Professor said, "Well, I'm glad I didn't sit in."

"I hit a lucky streak," Clint said.

"I might have folded to that pat hand," Smith said.

"Except that I had to make my play first," Clint said. "But with three sixes it didn't matter where I was sitting. I had to play them."

"And you filled with those eights."

Clint nodded and said, "That's luck."

"Let's hope your luck holds in everything."

Chapter Thirty-Seven

The Alhambra had its own dining room, so they decided to stay there and eat.

"Could you play poker for a living?" Smith asked, when they were seated.

"No," Clint said.

"Why not?"

"I don't have the patience," Clint said. "You've got to be willing to play every day, all day, for hours at a time if need be."

"Like Cody and Gallagher?"

"Cody, maybe," Clint said. "Gallagher's not as good as he thinks."

"Then I guess you showed him that."

Clint's eyes scanned the room.

"See anybody?" Smith asked.

"No. Nobody right now," Clint said. "I think we can eat in peace."

So they ordered, a steak dinner for Clint, chicken for Smith, who seemed to prefer it.

"You don't know *anything* about Hassan," Clint said, while they ate.

"No," Smith said. "He said he's worked for my uncle for two years. I didn't know anything about it."

"Well, if he doesn't find us, we're going to want to find him, right?"

"But how do we do that?"

"We get into your uncle's house," Clint said. "Maybe there's something there that will tell us where to find him."

Smith snapped his fingers.

"The smaller house behind the big one," he said. "That's where we look."

"Good thinking," Clint said. "We can check it after supper."

"Why not wait 'til morning, when it's light?"

"We can light a lamp," Clint said. "They might be watching the house. If they see a light, it might draw them out."

"So we're going there to try and find him, or have him find us."

"Right."

"I think next time we see him, or his boys," Smith said, "you should just shoot them."

"Well," Clint said, "maybe all but one."

Chapter Thirty-Eight

Clint didn't know how to find Rufus, so they simply walked outside the hotel and had the doorman get them a cab. After giving the driver the address, Clint said, "And we'll need you to wait."

The driver, a man in his forties, shrugged and said, "As long as yer payin' me, yer the boss."

It was fully dark by the time they arrived at the big house.

"This is the place?"

"This is it."

"The law was here—yesterday, was it?"

"We know," Clint said. "It should be empty now."

"If yer lookin' to steal stuff, ya can't put it in my cab," the man said.

"What's your name?"

"Jackson."

"We're not stealing anything, Jackson," Clint said. "We're just looking around. So we need you to wait for us." He handed Jackson some money.

"Okay," Jackson said, "I'll wait."

Clint and Smith made their way up the driveway.

"Who will the house go to now that he's dead?" Clint asked.

"I don't know," Smith said. "He's got no other family."

"Would he have left it to a servant?"

"Maybe Lem," Smith said, "but he's dead, too."

"What about Hassan?"

"I don't think he'd leave it to a servant who's only worked for him for two years."

"And what about you?"

"Me?" The question seemed to never have occurred to him. "I suppose that's a possibility."

They stopped in front of the main door.

"Then why not wait and see?" Clint asked. "If the house and everything in it is yours, you could turn it all into plenty of money to fund your trips."

"It would take a while," Smith said, "and I'm ready to go now. But if it does happen, I could leave it in the hands of a lawyer."

"Yeah, you could," Clint agreed. "Let's go around back and check the small house first."

They circled the big house, which was completely dark inside, but when they reached the back they could see a light in the small house.

"Well," Clint whispered, "somebody's home."

"Let's go see who it is," Smith said, and started forward.

Clint grabbed his arm to stop him.

"Slow," he said. "We don't want to go running into a whole nest of thugs, do we?"

"Good thinking," Smith said.

"Let's just take a look through a window first."

Calling the house "small" was just when compared to the main house. This one still had six rooms or so, spread out on one floor.

They moved silently toward the window the light was coming from. It turned out it wasn't just a window, but a set of French doors. Each set was covered with filmy white curtains, which they were able to see through.

They each stood off to one side and peered in a door. Five men in turbans, sat on the floor around what looked like a small altar. One of the men was Hassan.

"There he is," Smith said. "Are we going in?"

"We could," Clint said, "or we could wait for him to come out. If we do that, we might only have to deal with him."

"So which way do we go?" Smith asked.

"Let's just wait and see."

Chapter Thirty-Nine

After about an hour, it looked like the gathering was going to break up. Unfortunately, it also appeared that all five men were going to leave together.

"Now what?" Smith asked. "If they leave at the same time—"

"—we follow Hassan," Clint said. "Let's find out where he's living."

"What about Jackson?" Smith asked. "Will they see him when they leave?"

"No, he's far enough down the street," Clint said. "In fact, we better get back to him."

"Are we going to be able to pick Hassan out when they leave?"

"He's the tallest," Clint said. "We can go with that."

"Okay."

They turned, moved away from the house, made their way around to the front of the big house, down the driveway and back to Jackson, who was dozing in the back of his cab.

"Jackson!" Clint shook him.

"Huh? Wha—"

"Some men are coming out," Clint said. "We're going to follow one of them."

J.R. Roberts

"Okay." Jackson wiped his face with both hands. "Just tell me who."

***

They waited ten minutes, and then four bearded men with turbans came around from behind the house and up the driveway. When they got to the street they started walking.

"Where's Hassan?" Smith wondered aloud.

"Maybe he's not leaving," Clint said. "Maybe he's living there."

"Do you think the police would let him?" Smith asked.

"I don't know," Clint said. "If they questioned him, and can't connect him to the murders, maybe."

They waited a while longer, then Clint said, "We've got to go back in."

"Want me to wait?" Jackson asked.

"Yes, please," Smith said.

"No problem," the driver said. "Just wake me when you come back out."

He was climbing back into the cab when they started for the house.

***

168

As they approached the smaller house again Clint said, "No light."

"That's not good," Smith said. "If he didn't go out the front, where'd he go?"

"There's probably a back way."

"So he knew we were waiting?" Smith asked.

"Maybe he was just being careful."

"Well . . . should we go in?" Smith asked. "Like we were going to? We might find something to—"

"Look!" Clint hissed, pointing at the big house.

Smith turned and saw what Clint was pointing at. There was now a light in the big house.

"He's in there!" Smith said.

"It's got to be him," Clint said.

"I can understand if the police let him live in this house," Smith said, "but that one?"

"Maybe they don't know," Clint said.

"Are we going in there and find out what the hell is going on?"

"We are," Clint said, "but let's do it quietly."

"Lead the way," Smith said.

***

They approached the large house from the back, rather than the front. The light they were seeing was up on the second floor.

"So what do we do, climb in a window?" Smith whispered.

"Back door," Clint said. "Most people don't put as good a door on the back as they do the front."

They walked to the back door, where Clint tried the doorknob.

"Locked," Smith said.

"That's what we expected," Clint said. "Let's see what I can do."

"Should I stand watch?"

"There's nobody back here," Clint said. "Just stand by."

In the past Clint had opened many back doors by applying pressure. Most of them just popped open. Not this one. It was going to take a little more.

"Problems?"

"It's just going to take longer," Clint said. "I'm trying to do this quietly."

"Break the glass," Smith said.

"That's noise, Professor."

"Not from upstairs," Smith said. "Just pop the corner of it, so you can stick your hand in."

"You've done this before?" Clint asked.

"Once or twice," Smith said. "Change places with me."

Chapter Forty

Smith cracked the glass in the lower right-hand corner, by tap-tap-tapping it until it starred, using the butt of a knife he carried.

"Easy," Clint said.

"I'm just going to ease the tip of the knife into this crack, and then I can make the broken glass fall out, not in." He demonstrated, and caught most of the glass fragments in his hand before they could hit the ground. He missed a few shards, but they didn't make much noise when they fell.

Smith set the broken pieces down on the ground, reached in through the hole and unlocked the door.

"There you go," he said. "Don't step on the glass."

He opened the door and went inside, with Clint behind him.

Inside Clint said, "You don't have your gun."

"No, I left it in my room."

"Then let me go first."

"Be my guest," Smith said.

Clint moved ahead of Smith, and the two of them moved slowly through the dark house. As they did, they heard the ceiling above them creak. Clint pointed up and Smith nodded.

When they reached the stairs, Smith reached out and touched Clint on the shoulder.

"Why don't we just wait for him to come down?" he asked.

"We waited for him to come out, and he never did," Clint reminded him. "What if he doesn't come down?"

Smith nodded, waved at Clint to go ahead and lead the way up the stairs. They could only hope that none of the steps would creak the way the floor above them was.

Clint started up the stairs, keeping to one side because stairs usually creaked right at the center. Smith saw what he was doing, so he started up the stairs, keeping to the opposite side. When they reached the top Clint pointed down the hall to the right, where the light was emanating from. Smith nodded, and they started to creep down the hall.

As they got closer to the room the light was coming from, they heard sounds of somebody moving around, a sound that could have been furniture being moved, drawers being opened and closed.

When they got to the door Clint signaled to Smith to wait, and then moved to peer in the doorway. He expected to see Hassan moving around the room, but instead he saw a tall, blond woman who seemed to be ransacking the room. As she literally pulled the mattress off the bed,

Clint signaled to Smith to have a look. When he did, he looked at Clint and shrugged.

Professor Smith had no idea who the woman was, so the two men decided to step into the room and find out.

Chapter Forty-One

As Clint and Professor Smith stepped into the room, the blonde woman turned, saw them and stopped.

"Who the hell are you?" she demanded, glaring at them.

She was beautiful, but to Clint she looked like an Amazon. She had to be six feet tall, with a mass of blonde hair falling to her shoulders. She was wearing a man's shirt and trousers, and a pair of heavy boots.

"We were about to ask you the same thing," Smith said to her.

"I asked you first," she said, pointing at Clint, "and if you think that gun's gonna scare me—"

"Nobody's trying to scare you," Clint said. "I'm Clint Adams, this is Professor Henry Smith."

"You're Smith?" she asked, looking at him.

"That's right."

"Professor Smith?"

"Should I know you?" he asked.

"My name is Bliss, Charlotte Bliss."

Clint thought the woman was speaking as if Smith should know her, so he waited.

"You're Bliss?" Smith asked.

"That's right," she said. "And if you know what's good for you, Smith, you'll tell me where it is."

"I'm guessing you know who she is," Clint said to Smith.

"She's an archeologist."

"You mean . . . the female version of you?"

"Please!" Bliss said. "He wishes he was the male version of me."

"Charlotte, what are you doing here?" Smith demanded.

"You know what I'm doing here, Professor," she said. "Where is it?"

"What is she talking about?" Clint asked.

"Wait!" Smith said. "Charlotte, is Hassan here?"

"Hassan? I haven't seen him."

"Did you kill Everett?"

"Kill-what? Did I kill him? No, I worked for him."

"What?"

"That's right," Charlotte said. "He gave me jobs to do, all around the world. Then I came back and he paid me. This time he was supposed to pay me with—never mind. You don't know, do you?"

"Look," Clint said, "I suggest we take this downstairs, maybe have a drink."

She looked around the room she'd been ransacking, then said, "That sounds like a good idea."

***

"So you're Clint Adams, the Gunsmith?" Charlotte asked.

They were downstairs in Everett Anderson's library, where there was also a bar.

"I thought that was just a legend."

"Sometimes I wish it was," Clint said.

Smith came over and handed them each a glass of whiskey.

"So what were you looking for, Miss Bliss?" Clint asked.

"You can call me Charlotte," she said, "and none of your business. What were you two doing here?"

"Looking for Hassan," Clint said. "We were going to try to find out who killed Anderson."

"What made you think Hassan was in here?"

"He was in the smaller house in the back with some of his thug buddies," Clint said. "Then they left, but we saw the light in here. We thought it was him."

"Are we talking thuggees?" she asked.

"Yes, we are," Smith said.

She made a face.

"I hate those bastards!"

"So do I," Smith said.

"So who ransacked the collection?" she asked.

"That was done by whoever killed Anderson," Clint said.

"Not me!" Charlotte said.

"We understand that," Clint said. "You're here looking for an item Anderson was going to give you as payment for a job."

"Right."

"Do you want to tell us what that item is?" Clint asked. "In case we come across it."

"No."

"Whatever it was," Smith said. "it must have been in the collection room. What were you doing upstairs?"

"When I saw what a mess the room was, I thought maybe he might have hidden it somewhere else."

"In one of the spare bedrooms?"

"I checked *all* the bedrooms," she said. "You caught me in the last one."

"So you've looked everywhere?" Smith asked.

"Oh," she said, "I'm sure there are some nooks I haven't gotten to, yet."

"So you'd like us to just leave you here to finish up?" Clint asked.

"Yes," she said, regarding him over the rim of her glass, "but maybe we can do something together later?"

"Like what?" Clint asked.

"Oh, use your imagination, Mr. Gunsmith."

Chapter Forty-Two

Clint and Smith woke Jackson and had him drive them back to the Bella Union.

"That was a waste of time," Smith complained. "I guess we should've broken in on Hassan and his men when we saw them."

"Five against two?" Clint asked.

"Your gun against their swords," Smith said. "I'd bet on you."

"Then we would've had five dead thugs and the law all over us," Clint said. "They might've kept us tied up so long you'd miss your freighter."

"Okay, then," Smith said. "What's next?"

"Hassan must've been meeting with his boys for a reason," Clint said. "I think the reason was probably to send them after us."

"And if he does?"

"We keep at least one of them alive to lead us to Hassan," Clint said.

"So we kill the other three?"

"If we have to."

"I don't think they'll give us a choice," Smith said. "I guess I better start carrying my gun."

"I think you better."

***

When they got to the Bella Union, they went to Smith's room to get his gun. He had a military holster with a flap on it, which he strapped on.

"I'm still impressed by that gun," Clint said.

"Maybe before this is over, I'll give you a chance to shoot it," Smith said. "I'd love to see it in the hand of somebody who can really shoot."

They left Smith's room and went down to the lobby. From there they entered the Bella Union saloon, went to the bar and got a beer.

"Are we going to stay up all night, waiting?" Smith asked Clint.

"I think they'll come for us in the dark."

"So where do we hide?"

"They know we're here, at the Bella Union, and they probably know what rooms we're in."

"So we pick one of the rooms and wait in it?" Smith asked.

"Yes."

"Which one?" Smith asked. "Yours or mine?"

Clint finished his beer and said, "Neither."

***

Rather than try to recruit another hotel manager, they simply registered in a third room. Since the clerk on duty didn't know who Clint was, he signed the register with a phony name. They went up to the room, which was down the hall from their two.

"Leave the door open a crack," Clint said, "and let's take turns watching."

"All right," Smith said, "I'll go first. You get some rest."

So they split their time between being on watch at the door, and using the bed, waiting for Hassan's thugs to put in an appearance.

Chapter Forty-Three

When Smith touched Clint's shoulder he was instantly awake.

"Somebody's down the hall," Smith whispered.

Clint came off the bed immediately. He hadn't bothered to remove his holster.

"Let's go."

They left the room and crept down the hall. The door to Clint's room was ajar.

"Wait," Clint said. "Let's let them come out."

But nobody came out. Then Clint noticed the scent in the air.

"Oh," he said.

"What?"

"It's not them."

"Who is it, then?"

"I'll go in and find out," Clint said. "You go back to the other room, keep the door cracked, and keep watch."

"You sure?"

"I'm sure."

Smith shrugged, turned and went back up the hall.

Clint stepped to the door, again breathed in the perfume, realized he'd smelled it once before, and entered the room. As he did someone turned up the lamp. In the glow of the light he saw the woman seated on the bed.

"I told you we'd do something together," Charlotte Bliss said.

She was wearing the same clothes, but the shirt now had a couple of buttons undone. He could see the swell of her breasts as she leaned back on her hands.

"You shouldn't be here," he said.

"Why not?" she asked. "You're not married, are you? Even if you are—"

"No," Clint said, "no wife, just a bunch of thugs coming to kill me."

She sat up straight. "Oh." She looked around.

"But I'm all in favor of us doing something together," he said, "just at another time."

"Well," she said, standing up, "I suppose that'll have to do."

Suddenly, the window broke and a knife came hurtling through. It imbedded itself in Charlotte's back and she went down. Her body was so loose when it struck the floor that he knew she was dead.

Clint threw himself on the floor, rolled, came up near the lamp and blew it out.

He knew there was a building across the way, but it was pretty far. For someone to throw a knife from that distance, with that accuracy, was uncanny. Or, as Smith might say, it was thuggee.

"Clint!" The voice was Smith's, coming from the hall. "Stay back!"

"Clint!"

Then he realized, Smith wasn't calling out to check on him, or warn him, he was calling for help.

He scrambled along the floor to the door, and out into the hall. Up the hall Smith was struggling with two men. Since he knew how adept the professor was at handling himself, the fact that he was having trouble meant the two men were at least his equal. Two equals equaled an advantage.

He didn't know why Smith hadn't drawn his gun, but he drew his and fired. One of the men yelled and spun around, then hit the floor. That left Smith to deal with the other man, which he did. In one swift movement, he snapped the man's neck. As he dropped him to the floor, Clint ran to his side.

"We need one alive," he reminded Smith. "There are probably two more outside."

"How do we get them inside?"

"We don't," Clint said. "We go out. Where's your gun?"

"In the room, on the floor. Who was in your room?"

"Charlotte."

"Wha—"

"She's dead."

"Let me get my gun," Smith said, starting back into his room.

"Forget it," Clint said. "Let's get outside." He didn't want to chance another knife coming through a window.

As they ran down the stairs to the lobby, Smith asked, "What makes you think they didn't run off?"

"They're here to do a job," Clint said. "I don't think they're going to leave until they do it, or get killed trying."

"Let's hope they do," Smith said.

***

Outside on the street they stopped.

"Now what?"

"The alley," Clint said, "between our hotel and the next one. That's the building they threw the knife from that killed Charlotte."

"Then shouldn't we go in that building?"

"They won't be there," Clint said. "Let's go into the alley."

They left the street and moved toward the alley.

"It's dark in there," Smith said.

"That's how they're going to like it."

"Yeah, but—"

"It doesn't matter how dark it is," Clint said. "if somebody's moving around, you can see them—feel them."

"If you say so."

"Just stay behind me."

"I wish I had my gun," Smith said.

Clint was actually glad that the professor was *not* behind him with a gun.

They moved into the alley, slowly. The remaining thugs—and Clint hoped there was only two of them—were there. He could feel it.

And they were good. Before Clint knew it, he felt somebody behind them. When he turned, there was a man behind Smith, holding a knife to his throat. Clint's eyes were used to the darkness, so he could make out two figures, Smith and the thug. That left one more.

"You will come with us," the man said.

"Sure," Clint said, "just tell me where your friend is."

The man smiled, showing a mass of white teeth, and once again Clint felt someone behind him. He turned, drawing as he did, and fired once into the darkness. He heard a grunt, and then the sound of a body falling. Then he turned back to the other one.

"That leaves you," he said. "Your friends inside are dead." Clint gave the man the opportunity to realize he was the last one. He looked behind him, could see prone figure on the ground. "So's this one."

"You kill me," Smith said, with the knife blade to his throat, "my friend kills you."

"It's your call," Clint said.

After a few moments the man wet his lips and asked, "What do you want?"

"Well, for starters, take the knife away from his throat," Clint said.

The man obeyed, releasing Smith.

"Now drop it."

He did.

"Let's get out of this alley, to where there's more light," Clint said.

The three of them walked to the mouth of the alley. The man looked dejected behind his black beard. He reached up and removed the turban. Maybe he thought he didn't deserve to wear it, anymore.

"All right," Clint said, "now where's Hassan?"

"He is at the house of Mr. Anderson," the man said.

"Now, we saw all of you in the smaller house," Clint said. "Then four of you left. Where did Hassan go?"

"Into the main house."

"We didn't see him leave."

"There is a secret passageway beneath the two houses, that connects them."

That would explain why they never saw Hassan leave the property.

"So we were in the damn house and didn't see him," Smith said, shaking his head.

"There are many places in that big house to hide," the man said. "He is there, waiting for us to come back and tell him we killed you."

That meant Hassan was there while they had been talking to Charlotte Bliss.

"Do you believe him?" Smith asked Clint.

They both studied the man.

"It is true!" he told them.

"Yeah, I believe him," Clint said.

"Then you will let me go?" the man asked them, his tone hopeful.

"I don't think so. There's a dead woman in the hotel," Clint said, "and three dead men inside and outside. No, we won't let you go. But we won't kill you. We'll turn you over to the law."

"And then we'll go and visit Hassan," Smith said.

Chapter Forty-Four

Detectives Saunders and Lauderbach responded when the hotel manager sent word to the San Francisco Police Department that there were dead bodies in his hotel.

"Mr. Adams," Saunders said, when he saw Clint in the lobby. "Don't tell me you're involved in this little shoot-out?"

"Not just a shoot-out," Clint said. "Somebody threw a knife through my window into a friend's back—a female friend."

"And were you the intended target?"

"Probably."

"And does this have anything to do with the murder of Everett Anderson and his man servant?"

"I don't know," Clint said. "All I know is somebody tried to kill me tonight."

"And you killed them, instead."

"All but one," Clint said. "We saved him for you."

"We?"

Clint pointed across the lobby, where Professor Smith was sitting with the surviving attacker.

"Okay," Saunders said, "don't go away."

"I'm not going anywhere," Clint promised.

***

Saunders and Lauderbach went to the second floor to look at Charlotte Bliss' body, and the bodies of the two thugs. Then they went to the alley to see the third man. That done, they had the bodies removed, and talked to the surviving man.

Once they put their prisoner into a horse-drawn wagon, the detectives joined Clint and Smith in the lobby.

"We're going to need the two of you to come to our office and make statements."

"We'll be right behind you, Detective," Clint promised.

"You better be," Saunders said. "Don't make us come looking for you."

"We'll be there as soon as we get a cab."

Saunders and Lauderbach left the lobby, and Smith turned to Clint.

"As soon as we get a cab?" he asked.

"Give or take an hour or two," Clint said. "Hopefully, when we do show up at their office, we'll have Hassan with us and be able to explain everything."

"Alive?"

"I hope so."

"Well," Smith said, "just in case, I'm going to my room to get my gun."

Clint almost told him he would wait in the lobby for him but thought better of it.

"I'll come with you."

Chapter Forty-Five

Jackson drove Clint and Smith back to the Anderson house.

"Am I waitin' again?" he asked.

"Yes," Clint said. "If it goes well, we'll be coming out with somebody we want to take to the police. Do you have a problem with that?"

"No, no problems with the police. Not me."

"Good," Clint said. "Hopefully, this won't take long."

"Wouldn't you rather do this in the daylight?" Jackson asked.

"No," Clint said, "we want to get this done now."

"Okay," Jackson said, climbing into the cab. "Wake me when you need me."

Clint and Smith headed for the house.

"I hope Hassan's still in there," the Professor said.

"That's why I want to do this tonight," Clint said. "He's waiting to hear from his people before he decides to move."

Once again they let themselves in the back door, where Smith had already broken the glass.

Clint put his hand on Smith's shoulder.

"Let's go in easy," he said. "We don't know if Hassan found this broken glass, or not."

Smith nodded, took his European gun from his holster.

"Don't shoot unless I do," Clint warned him.

"Okay."

They walked through the dining room, didn't hear any sounds from upstairs as they had the first time. Also, there was no light.

"Think he's gone?" Smith asked.

"I hope not," Clint said. "Let's check the secret passage."

"Where did that man say it was?"

"The library."

They found the hall that led to the library. Once in the room Clint lit the lamp on the desk.

"Is that wise?" Smith asked.

"Is any of this?" Clint asked. "If he's down below, he won't see it."

Clint walked to the set of shelves the thug had told him about, hoping the man hadn't lied. He hadn't. With just a little pressure, the shelf moved, revealing a doorway. Inside an oil lamp was on a hook. Next to it was an empty hook.

"He's down there," Clint said, taking the lamp from the hook. He lit it, held it out in front of him, saw the stairway leading down.

"Are you ready?" he asked Smith.

"I've been in a lot of secret passages, remember?" Smith asked. "I'm ready."

They started down the steps.

"The thug said there was a secret passage from here to the smaller house," Smith commented. "He didn't say if there was anything else down here."

"Well, we're going to find out."

When they reached the bottom of the steps, they saw a light ahead of them for the first time.

"*Somebody's* here," Smith said.

Clint waved at him to keep quiet as they worked their way along the passage.

As they got closer to the light, they heard a voice, not talking, but chanting. Closer still to the light Clint blew out his own lamp and set it down on the ground.

As they reached the light, they saw that they were in a cavern, a man seated on the floor had his back to them. A look around revealed the cavern to otherwise be empty, no furniture at all.

"Come in, sahibs," Hassan said, not bothering to turn. "I have been expecting you."

Clint and Smith entered the cavern.

"Turn around with your hands empty, Hassan," Clint said.

Hassan immediately spread his hands to show they were empty, then got to his feet and turned. He then folded his hands and bowed.

"Welcome."

"Never mind being polite," Smith said. "You killed Everett, didn't you, Hassan?"

"Not with these hands," Hassan said, showing his empty hands again, "but yes, I had him killed. Am I correct in assuming that you have killed my men?"

"Three of them" Clint said. "The fourth one is talking to the law."

"That is a shame," Hassan said. "I would have preferred you kill all four."

"Sorry to disappoint you," Clint said.

"Let's go," Smith said, brandishing his gun.

"Where?"

"We're turning you over to the police," Smith said. "I'd rather shoot you dead where you stand, but Clint wants you to pay for your crimes."

"My crimes?" Hassan said. "I have committed no crimes."

"Uncle Everett is dead," Smith said, "Lem is dead, and Charlotte Bliss is dead."

"But I did not kill any of them."

"What do you have there?" Clint asked, indicating where Hassan had been sitting when they entered.

The bearded, turbaned man stepped aside, revealing what looked like a small altar in the center of the room, with something burning. Also on the altar were some of the items Smith had shown Clint in the collection room—the cursed items.

"Who were you putting a curse on, Hassan?" Smith asked.

"I am afraid it was you, sahib," Hassan said. "We cannot have you going to the Gold City without a curse."

"Like the one that killed my father?"

"Alas," Hassan said, "I am much too young to re-member the curse that killed your father. I am only concerned with killing you."

"But you don't have the gall to do it yourself, is that it?" Smith asked.

"Actually," Hassan said, "that is not it, at all."

Suddenly, moving very quickly, he pulled a knife from his sleeve and threw it. The move completely surprised Smith, but not Clint. He reached out with his left hand to push Smith out of the way, and with his right drew his gun and fired.

The bullet struck Hassan in the chest. He looked down at the blood that blossomed there, then looked at Clint and seemed puzzled. He coughed then, and a great gout of blood poured from his mouth, creating a puddle at his feet that he then slumped into.

"Jesus!" Smith swore. "I didn't even see him draw it."

"I did," Clint said, holstering his gun.

"How do we explain this to the detectives?" Smith asked. "We were going to bring him in alive."

Clint looked at the knife that was sticking in his left forearm and said, "I don't think we'll have any trouble with a plea of self-defense."

Smith turned, started to speak, then saw the knife.

"Jesus!" he said, again.

***

After they removed the knife and bound the wound tightly, to stem the flow of blood, Clint insisted on searching the small house first.

"You need a doctor," Smith said.

"After we're done, here. You still want to find out how your father was killed, right?"

"You think there's something here?"

"I think it's worth a look."

***

With Clint leaking blood along the way, they moved on to the small house and did a quick search. It did look like Hassan was living there; his clothing was in the chest of drawers in the bedroom. There was, however, nothing to indicate that Hassan was thuggee.

"We might be better off not even mentioning that to the police," Clint said. "It would take a lot of explaining."

"So Hassan and his bunch were just killers?"

"The law can believe that," Clint said, looking at his arm.

Chapter Forty-Six

"So the freighter left without us?" Clint asked.

"I'm afraid so," Smith said. "I felt I had to stay around for the reading of Everett Anderson's will."

"And when was that?" Clint asked.

"Yesterday."

It had been several days since Clint and Smith made their statement to the police, after calling them to the Anderson house to pick up Hassan's body. The detectives were not happy with the appearance of another dead body, but Clint had been right about the knife in his arm. It helped legitimize their story.

Now they were sitting in the Bella Union's saloon, catching up.

"And?" Clint asked.

"He wasn't really my uncle, you know," Smith said.

"He didn't leave you his house?"

Smith shook his head and said, "Or his money. Some of the artifacts he knew I'd like, though. So I guess I'm satisfied with that."

"And the house and money?"

"To charity."

"So now what?"

"There's a freighter leaving for India in a week," Smith said. "I'll be on it."

"Still intent on finding out how the curse of the Gold City killed your father?"

"I'm not about to give that quest up," Smith said.

"You know," Clint said, "I don't really know all that much about your father's death."

"That's the problem," Smith said. "We never did find out a lot about it. He died while in India, near the Pakistani border. His body was shipped home—oh, this was over ten years ago. I was still in the university. All we ever heard was that his death had to do with a curse. My mother never believed it. She died a few years later."

"And you believed it?"

"I looked into it," Smith went on. "Found out there actually was a Curse of the Gold City. But somehow, I never got there. Recently, I've started to think what a lousy son I was, never going there to find out what really happened."

"Isn't it possible it's too late?"

Smith laughed.

"You're talking to a man who investigates mysteries that are thousands of years old."

Clint also laughed.

"You're right, of course."

"You're still invited, you know."

"I think I've had enough of men in turbans with scimitars for a while," Clint said. "Besides, I can't just sit around and wait a week."

"What about your poker game?"

"Oh, I played the last few nights," Clint said. "It's over."

"Did you win?"

Clint shook his head.

"Al Cody was the big winner," he said. "That was no surprise."

"So what have you been doing?"

Clint thought about Alexandra, still up in his room. She had knocked on his door the night before and reminded him of her warning that "he might be next." But he thought it better not to mention that to Smith.

"And now?"

"I'll be on the next train out tomorrow," Clint said. "Time for me to get back in my saddle."

Coming April 27, 2019

THE GUNSMITH
446
Deadville City

For more information
visit: www.SpeakingVolumes.us

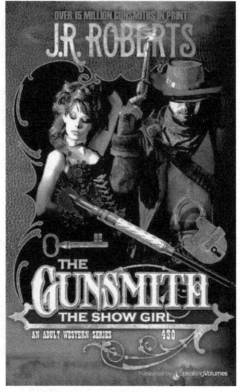

Coming Spring 2019

Lady Gunsmith 7
Roxy Doyle and the James Boys

**For more information
visit**: www.SpeakingVolumes.us

On Sale Now!

Lady Gunsmith *series*
Books 1-6

**For more information
visit:** www.SpeakingVolumes.us

On Sale Now!

TRACKER *series*
by
**Award-Winning Author
Robert J. Randisi (J.R. Roberts)**

On Sale Now!

MOUNTAIN JACK PIKE *series*
by
Award-Winning Author
Robert J. Randisi (J.R. Roberts)

For more information
visit:

CPSIA information can be obtained
at www.ICGtesting.com
Printed in the USA
LVHW051428120720
660450LV00002BA/217

9 781645 400059